She closed her eye[...]
her bare skin, hungry k[...]
As quickly as it came, [...]
butter on a summer sidewalk. When she o[...]
eyes, the man was staring straight at her, as if reading her thoughts. She felt an immediate jolt of heat and couldn't look away. He stood and started walking toward her.

If he asked her to dance, she wouldn't say no. If he took her hand, she wouldn't pull away. If he wanted her to run away with him, she would.

He placed one booted foot on the chair beside her and leaned on his bent knee, close enough to be intimate, but not too close to feel threatening. His smile held her captive, making her feel as if she'd done something wicked. Or would if she didn't break the spell he had over her. When he spoke, his voice was everything she might have imagined, soft and bluesy, as if it just needed a bass guitar to be complete. "Hey, Ruby."

Her body responded before her brain could make sense of it. She felt a spark, a tingle, a molten heat. "You must have me confused with someone else," she said, but her voice was shaky. "My name is Meg."

He tipped his head and smiled. "My mistake."

Also by Wild Rose Press…

The Magic Christmas Box
East of Easy

Book Awards:
Eppie Awards
Royal Palm Literary Award
Dorothy Parker Reviewers Choice
Dream Realm Award

Not Her Story

by

Linda Bleser

Not Her Story

Cover Art by *Kim Mendoza*

The Wild Rose Press, Inc.
PO Box 708
Adams Basin, NY 14410-0708
Visit us at www.thewildrosepress.com

Publishing History
First Edition, 2023
Trade Paperback ISBN 978-1-5092-4778-3
Digital ISBN 978-1-5092-4779-0

Published in the United States of America

Dedication

This book is dedicated to a dear friend whose experience with amnesia raised the question—how does our past define us and what happens when all our memories are erased?

****

I'd also like to acknowledge my friend and minister at All Paths to God, Rev. Sue Meixner, whose sermon "His Story" inspired this fictional story.

Chapter One

Twenty-three Years Ago, Tinder Falls, Connecticut

Megan Rose couldn't spell the word F-E-A-R yet, but she knew it well. Fear smelled sour, like her father's breath late at night. It tasted coppery, like blood on her tongue. Fear was the inward rush of a held breath as footsteps stopped outside the bedroom door. Fear felt like walking on slippery ice.

Although she was only five years old, Megan knew that fear could change a person forever.

She sat up in bed, clutching Sunny Bunny to her chest. Her nightlight cast a soft glow but couldn't reach the lurking shadows. The yelling had woken her. Her mother's voice pleading, her father's loud and sharp, anger spitting like hot sparks from a fire.

Something heavy hit the wall and crashed to the floor in a shower of breaking glass, followed by a thud and a scream. Megan covered her ears but couldn't block out the sounds of violence. She should have been used to it by now. Her parents often fought, but it was worse when they'd been drinking.

After a while, Megan heard angry footsteps clomping down the hall, then the front door slammed hard. Outside a car started up with a jerk and a shudder, followed by the squeal of tires.

She pulled Sunny Bunny close. Fear lessened its

grip on her throat. Her father was gone. And maybe, just maybe, he'd stay gone for good.

Megan heard her mother calling, climbed out of bed, and rushed into her parent's room. Her mother was on the floor, clutching her belly. There was blood. So much blood.

"Get the phone," her mother gasped. "Call 911 like we practiced." A low moan escaped her mouth. "Tell them to hurry. The baby's coming." She let out another cry. "Hurry, Meg!"

Megan knew all her numbers. Except sometimes she confused six and nine. One was right-side up and the other was upside down. But she grabbed the phone, took a deep breath, and got the numbers right the first time.

"911, what is your emergency?" The lady on the phone sounded nice, like Megan's kindergarten teacher.

"My mom's bleeding real bad. She said to hurry, the baby is coming."

"How old are you, hon?"

"I'm five," Megan said. "But I got the numbers right."

"The numbers?"

"The 911 numbers."

"You sure did, sweetie. You did real good. Is there anyone else with you besides your mother?"

"No. My dad was here, but he got really mad and left. Is someone coming to help my mother?"

"Yes, they're on the way with an ambulance. I'm going to need you to open the door when they get there, okay? But for now, I want you to stay on the phone with me."

And she did. The nice lady asked her about

kindergarten, and whether she liked Minnie Mouse more than Cinderella. Pretty soon Megan saw lights flashing outside the window and the lady told her she could hang up now and let the ambulance men in.

They came with a rolling bed and lifted her mother onto it. Meg wanted to go, but her mother said to stay there with her father.

"But he's…"

Her mother gave her a look that said she'd better do what she was told and not say a word about her father not being home or what had happened. Then her mother let out a cry that was all harsh and jagged, like broken glass, and one of the hospital men put a plastic mask over her face and they rushed her out the door.

The ambulance roared away, leaving Megan all alone. But she felt safer alone than if her father had been there. She closed and locked the door, even though it wouldn't keep her father out. He had a key.

When Megan woke up the next morning, her father still hadn't returned. It was a school day, but she didn't know how to get there by herself, so she turned on the cartoons, ate cereal right from the box, and wondered if her mother was all right. What if she was dead? And where was her father?

Then Megan discovered a new facet of fear. What if they were both dead-and-gone-to-heaven like Grandma Jean, and she was left all alone?

****

It wasn't until later that evening, as the room was getting dark, that she thought of the nice lady at the 911 place. Maybe she could help. But this time it was a different voice on the phone. A man. He asked a lot of questions then told Megan that someone would be coming to get her and bring her somewhere safe.

Chapter Two

Present Day

Who knew something as innocent as a Band-Aid could set a series of events into motion that would change everything?

Ben Tyler wasn't much of a handyman. His skills lay in words, images, scene, and sequel. But when he'd noticed an antique wooden cradle listed for sale on the college bulletin board, he couldn't resist buying it.

Of course, they wouldn't be needing the cradle for months, but he wanted to reassemble it and surprise Meg when she came home. He had a good feeling they'd be needing it soon. If his calculations were right, Meg was already late and could even now be carrying his future son or daughter. They'd been trying for so long, dealing with the disappointment and heartbreak every month when their dreams were once again crushed. But he had a good feeling this time.

The cradle would be a perfect surprise. It was light oak, with intricate scroll work lovingly carved, and it smelled of old wood and new life. Ben wondered how many babies had been rocked to sleep in it, and how many more would lay their heads here to rest once his own children outgrew it.

If only it had come fully assembled.

He searched through his meager supply of tools for

the right screwdriver but failed to find what he needed. Instead, he reached for his pocketknife. The tip fit perfectly in the little x-shaped groove. He pressed and twisted.

When the knife slipped, he didn't feel the pain right away. Just the blood flowing unchecked along the antique grain. Red, the color of rage, the color of lost hope and broken dreams.

Then the pain hit like a scream. He thrust his thumb into his mouth, tasted the blood and felt the sting. He closed his eyes and took a deep breath before removing his thumb to inspect the damage. Not too bad. It didn't look like he'd need stitches. Just needed to stop the flow of blood, that's all. Nothing a little Band-Aid wouldn't fix.

Wrapping his handkerchief around the wound, Ben made his way to the bathroom, but a search of the medicine chest turned up nothing but pill bottles and mouthwash. No Band-Aids. He searched a few more places they could be, and several places they shouldn't. Nothing.

Then he remembered Meg kept a small first-aid kit in her travel bag, along with a little sewing kit and travel-sized bottles of aspirin. That was his Meg. Always prepared for any little emergency.

He found the travel bag right where she always kept it, on the top shelf of her closet. He opened it up and frowned, unsure at first what he was looking at. Then it hit him. Three rows of pink pills and one row of white. Week one through four, each column labeled with the day of the week. Three blister packs full, one nearly empty.

Birth control pills. Meg was taking birth control

pills. Why? How long? He couldn't wrap his brain around the idea. They'd dreamed of the day they'd hold a child. They'd cried in each other's arms every month when her period came, dashing their hopes and dreams. They'd made plans, chosen names, and all this time…

Months. She'd been lying to him for months.

Ben set the birth control pills on the countertop, pulled up a bar stool and waited.

****

Meg loaded the grocery bags into the car with one hand and held the phone to her ear with the other. "I'm trying out a new cupcake recipe, Lucy. Tropical fruit with pineapple and coconut. I might call it Hawaiian Sunrise. Or maybe Tutti-Frutti like that gum you were obsessed with as a teenager."

She chuckled at her friend's response. "You were, too. Oh, and the flyers came in. They're gorgeous. I love the new logo."

With the last bag loaded, Meg slid behind the wheel and buckled her seatbelt. "Gotta run," she said. "I'll see you tonight." She blew an imaginary kiss into the phone, then hung up. Before she could put it back in her purse, however, the phone rang. The number was unfamiliar, and Meg almost let it go to voice mail, but changed her mind. It might be a new customer, and they could use all the orders they could get.

"Hello?"

There was no response, only silence on the other end. She was about to hang up when a song began playing. Shock, like a jolt of electricity traveled up her spine as she recognized the tune.

I'll make love to you.

Her breath caught in her throat, and she held the

phone out as if it was a bomb about to explode.

Like you want me to.

"No," she cried. Then louder as she disconnected the call. "No!"

A flurry of emotions rushed over her, one after the other—passion and pain, love and hate, betrayal and loss. And anger. Oh, so much anger. It surged up, raw and hot, the emotions as fresh as if it had happened yesterday.

When the phone rang again, she ignored it. She couldn't ignore the memories, however. Memories that sliced and burned. Memories that threw her back into a past that she'd tried her best to forget. She rested her forehead on the steering wheel and wept until there were no tears left. She'd sworn she'd never cry over a man again.

She was wrong.

Meg waited in the car until she was able to wrestle her emotions back under control. She checked her reflection in the rear-view mirror and wiped the tears from her eyes. She didn't want Ben to see she'd been crying. It would take too much explanation, and she couldn't lie. She was done lying to him.

****

Ben didn't have to wait long before Meg came in, balancing an armload of grocery bags. "I could use a little help here," she said.

He didn't budge, only watched her with disappointment and betrayal warring for control of his emotions.

She gave him a strange look and shook her head. "Fine." She leaned over and placed the bags on the countertop, then began unpacking. "They didn't have rye bread, so I bought pumpernickel instead. Oh, and look. English muffins were buy one, get one free." She turned, holding a package of English muffins in each hand, then spotted the birth control pills on the counter. She froze, blinked, looked at him, then away.

He watched her face as shock and guilt turned to anger. That's the way Meg handled conflict. She turned it outward and used anger as a weapon.

"What were you doing in my private things?"

"That's how you're going to play this, Meg?"

She turned away, setting the English muffins on the counter and lining them precisely, as she avoided his gaze.

"How long have we been *trying* to have a baby, Meg?" He stood and gripped her arm, turning her so she'd have to face him. "How long?"

"I don't know."

"I do. Fourteen months, Meg. Fourteen months of lies, pretending you wanted a baby as much as I did while all the time you were making sure we couldn't." He let out a half laugh. "You know what's funny? All this time I thought maybe it was my fault. Maybe I wasn't man enough to get you pregnant. And every month when we found out it wasn't going to happen, it broke my heart. Not just for myself, Meg, but for you. Because I'd let you down."

She turned away, but not before he saw the tears rolling down her face. "Why, Meg? Why would you lie to me about something so important?"

She shook her head. "You don't understand. You don't know what my life was like before I met you."

He tightened his grip on her shoulders. "Don't give me that crap. We've all been through unpleasant things, had disappointments and tragedies. That's no reason to lie."

Her eyes widened with fear. "Don't. Don't…"

He released his grip. She had to know he wouldn't hurt her. This was just another ploy to turn attention away from what she'd done. "You lied," he repeated. "That's the ultimate betrayal. I would never lie to you, Meg. *Never.*"

"It wasn't a lie," she said. "I needed time. I wasn't ready. There are things you don't understand."

"I don't understand because you don't share your feelings with me. You close up and brood. I'm sick and tired of your mood swings, your depression, your inability to let go of your past. Sick of it, Meg."

She turned away from him, a gentle tremor of her shoulders the only sign of emotion. Maybe she was sorry. Or maybe she was simply sorry she got caught.

"I thought a baby would change all that." Ben threw the packet of pills across the room. It hit the wall and bounced to the floor. Meg flinched as if she'd been struck. Ben turned and walked away. "I thought wrong."

Meg opened her mouth to call him back, but the words caught in her throat. Her hands clenched and unclenched. She wanted to trust Ben, to reveal everything about her dark past. But she couldn't. She couldn't bear to see the love in his eyes turn to disgust if he knew everything. She'd worked so hard to keep that part of her life hidden, even from herself.

Meg left the groceries on the counter, grabbed her keys, and walked out the door. She couldn't face Ben. Couldn't stand to see the hurt in his eyes. She should have told him everything, but she'd been afraid he'd leave if he knew what her life had really been like.

She'd thought that marrying someone safe, someone kind and gentle would chase her demons away, but if anything, it made her feel even more vulnerable. Maybe she would have told Ben everything if she wasn't so afraid he'd leave her like everyone else had.

So she drove, fast and mindless, her brain churning with guilt, shame, and half-forgotten pain.

With one hand on the steering wheel, she fumbled in her purse, found her cell phone, then hit redial. A shuddering breath caught in her throat. But no tears. She was fresh out of tears.

When a horn blared behind her, she looked up from the phone's display and swerved her car back onto the road. Her purse tumbled off the seat, contents spewing in every direction.

"Damn!"

Meg leaned over to grab her purse, unconsciously pulling the steering wheel in the same direction. When she looked up again, she was heading straight for a tree.

Too fast.

She pressed her foot on the brakes, but something had rolled and jammed beneath the pedal and she was going too fast, too damn fast.

Just before slamming into the tree, Meg heard a voice from her past answer the phone. But it was too late. She was hurtling at sixty miles an hour into an unknown future.

Chapter Three

There were no skid marks on the road.

Ben jerked awake, but the nightmare remained. He glanced at the hospital bed where Meg lay in a death-still coma. Her car had hit a solid oak tree at well over sixty miles an hour. An airbag saved her life, but the force of the impact had sent her brain slamming against the walls of her skull, leaving it swollen and bruised. She might never recover.

There were no skid marks.

The police officer's eyes had been filled with both accusation and pity. The words made no sense at first. Why was that important? Then he understood.

No skid marks.

Ben had refused to acknowledge the unasked question, preferring the catacomb silence of his own guilt. They didn't come out and say it, but Ben knew what they were implying. It wasn't just an accident. Meg had deliberately driven into that tree. *Suicide.* An ugly word. One he would never have used to describe Meg. Depressed, yes. Moody, more often than not. But suicidal? No, not Meg.

Then what about the fact that there were no skid marks?

Ben stood and stretched the kinks from his back. Two nights sleeping on a chair beside her bed had his body feeling like it was stitched together with barbed wire. But he couldn't leave. What if she woke up and he wasn't there?

He thought about the argument leading up to the accident, still angry that she'd lied to him. But now his anger was mixed with guilt. He should have made her stay, should have talked it out. Nothing was worth the risk of losing Meg.

Ben leaned over the bed and pressed his lips against her forehead, trying not to jostle the wires and tubes that were keeping her alive. "I won't leave, baby. I promise." Somehow, he knew that a whisper would be more likely to reach through the fog than a shout. Closing his eyes, he inhaled her scent, blotting out the hospital smells around him. It was easy to pretend, if only for a moment, that she was simply sleeping. But her skin was cold and clammy, as if her spirit had already fled.

He'd never seen her this still. Even in sleep she tossed and turned, kicked the covers, and cried out as if being chased. In the early years he'd tried to comfort her. He'd held her close and tight. But she'd fought against the prison of his arms. Lately he'd taken to sleeping on the couch, away from her kicking and whimpering.

Was she dreaming at all now, Ben wondered, or was she trapped in an endless void?

****

Megan dreams of walking home in a blizzard. The snow deepens, first surrounding her ankles and numbing her toes, then climbing to her knees, sucking her deeper with each step. She sees a wrought-iron gate up ahead and knows she has to reach it, even though she has no idea what lies past the railing. With a herculean effort, she pushes against the weight of snow, but the swirling mounds resist her efforts. Soon the snowdrifts reach her chest and just when she thinks she'll drown in a sea of snow, she's lifted up onto a pure-white wave. She rolls over, trying to find solid ground to stand on when the next snow wave comes and rolls her back again, drawing her further and further away. The gate is no longer visible in the sea of white, and she finally stops fighting. She rolls onto her back, stretches out her arms, and lets the swirling snowdrifts carry her away into a winter-white world.

****

A shadow fell over Meg's face. Ben looked up to see her best friend Lucy standing on the other side of the bed, her normally wild hair pulled into a severe bun, as if the situation was too somber for curls. As close as they were, Meg and Lucy were as different in their looks as in their personalities. Meg, dark-haired and mysterious, always looked as if she was about to tell you a secret, while Lucy, fair-skinned and freckled, with a mass of curly strawberry-blonde hair, had an open face and a quick smile.

"How's she doing?" Lucy asked.

"Same."

Lucy looked into Ben's eyes, then away. Lucy and Ben weren't close. The only thing they had in common was their love for Meg. Ben wondered if she'd been waiting for a reason to hate him.

"I don't blame you," Lucy said as if reading his thoughts. "Meg's been running from her demons for a long, long time." She shook her head slowly. "It's a wonder something like this hadn't happened sooner."

Then she looked Ben in the eye, and this time he saw a glimmer of understanding. "You were good for her."

"Not good enough." That's when he broke. Ben could have taken blame or accusations, but not compassion. He didn't deserve it. Not when Meg lay in a coma. Not when there was a chance she'd never be the same.

"You know what her life was like," Lucy said.

He did, in a distant kind of way. Meg rarely talked about her childhood. When she did, it was like talking about a book she'd read or a movie she'd seen. She told her story like a bystander watching the events unfold, showing little if any emotion. The real horrors lay below the surface, erupting in nightmare screams and thrashing feet.

He knew that she and Lucy had grown up together in an orphanage—St. Ophelia's Home for Girls. She wouldn't talk about what led to her being there or what her life was like before then. Whatever their life was like, it seemed Lucy hadn't escaped unscathed either. She was single with two bad marriages behind her and a constant stream of dead-end relationships.

"I was there," Lucy said, her dark eyes growing more distant. "I saw the bruises that she couldn't hide." She shrugged one shoulder. "St. Ophelia's was filled with kids who each had their own horror story." Lucy's gaze drifted away, as if remembering what tragedies had led her to St. Ophelia's. "Everyone's parents are different," she said with a sigh. "Like stray dogs. Some barked louder than others. Some growled. And others bit without warning. Some just ran off without a second glance."

Ben nodded with understanding. He'd remembered

hearing one of those TV gurus say that when you abuse a child, you kill the person they were meant to be. Ben didn't believe that. He knew Meg in all her sweetness, her generosity, her charm. They hadn't killed the person she was meant to be. That person was still there inside, hiding beneath the hurt and pain and anger.

Ben would give anything to erase the events that had crippled her and turned her world into a dark, inescapable place.

Lucy took a deep breath. "You should go home."

"I can't. What if she wakes up and I'm not here?"

Lucy settled in a chair on the other side of Meg's hospital bed. She pulled a book out of her bag and shifted into a comfortable position. "Go home, take a shower, and get some sleep."

"But…"

Lucy's voice was stern. "If Meg wakes up, I'll tell her you'll be right back." She glanced at Meg's still form, then back to Ben. "She won't, though. The doctors will keep her this way until her brain, um…until she's had a chance to heal."

Ben knew she was right, but guilt kept him rooted to the spot. "It's my fault," he said. "We had a fight," he admitted. "I found her birth control pills." He shook his head. "All this time I thought we were trying to have a baby and she's been on birth control. I just lost it."

Lucy held his gaze for a moment, then looked away.

Ben frowned. "You knew?"

Lucy rolled one shoulder and grimaced. "Look, she was afraid, that's all. She was working on it and would have come around eventually."

"Come around? Why couldn't she just tell me she was afraid? Why make a big deal about not being pregnant when that's what she pretended to want all along? If we had just talked about it, none of this would have happened. And Meg wouldn't be lying in a coma after…"

"After what? You don't honestly think she tried to kill herself, do you?" Lucy rolled her eyes. "Meg's dealt with a lot worse than this, believe me. It was an accident, that's all."

"But the police said…"

"I know what the police said." Lucy's voice rose in anger. "So what? Just because there were no skid marks doesn't mean she hit the tree on purpose. Maybe her brakes failed. Or maybe she passed out." Her voice broke. "She said 'I'll see you tonight.' She wouldn't say that if…" Lucy shrugged. "We won't know anything for certain until she wakes up and tells us what happened. Until then, you need to keep your strength up."

Her voice softened in resignation. "So go on home and come back in the morning refreshed."

"Yeah, okay." Ben leaned over and kissed Meg's forehead. He glanced at Lucy, unsure what to say. *Thank you? Take good care of her? Call me if…*

In the end, he just turned and walked away.

****

It wasn't until Ben walked through the exit that he realized how accustomed he'd become to the claustrophobic hospital scent of sickness and death.

He took a deep breath and filled his lungs with fresh summer air, surprised that the world continued spinning while Meg lay unconscious three floors above.

Here in the outside world, drivers fought for right-of-way, people went to work in the morning and walked their dogs in the evening. People who didn't drive their wives to suicide.

Ben's world would never be the same. His vocabulary had increased these past few days with words he'd never imagined would be part of it. Words like *traumatic brain injury* and *intracranial hemorrhage* and *medically induced coma*. It was hard to associate any of those words with the woman he'd promised to love for better or worse.

Instead of going straight home, Ben stopped the car on a quiet street. Call it morbid curiosity. Or maybe he needed to convince himself this was real, not some horrible nightmare he was trapped inside. He pulled over and stared at the spot where his life had been split in two, before and after.

Even two days later there was evidence of a life shattered—brittle shards of glass glistening under the street lamp's amber glow, scattered wood chips where a mighty oak had once stood, silently answering the question of what happened when an unstoppable force met an immovable object.

Traumatic brain injury. Intracranial hemorrhage. Medically induced coma.

That was what happened.

Ben's lips tightened. His hand curled into a tight fist and slammed once, twice, three times on the dashboard. *How could you, Meg? How the hell could you do this, dammit?*

In the safety of his car, Ben raged and screamed until the adrenalin drained from his body, leaving him limp and hopeless. Only then did he turn away from the scene of the accident and drive home. A home that was too empty and too quiet without the beep-beep of hospital monitors and the hush-hush of soft-soled nursing shoes and the drugged whimpers of sleeping patients. Much too quiet to cover up the guilt and blame he carried inside.

Ben turned on the TV to cut through the silence, then opened the refrigerator and stared inside until he realized he had no appetite. He slumped on the couch fully clothed to rest his eyes for just a moment and fell asleep almost instantly.

Chapter Four

Twenty Years Ago - St. Ophelia's Home for Girls

Meg had cried herself empty, but a thousand tears couldn't ease the pain inside. She felt alone, abandoned. No one cared if she lived or died. Sometimes she didn't care herself.

A shadow shifted in the darkened room. Meg blinked her eyes but saw only shades of gray. When a voice whispered soft and soothing in her ear, Meg thought she was dreaming.

"Don't cry. It'll be all right."

"You don't know that," Meg sobbed. "Nothing's ever gonna be all right. Not for me"

"No. You're just confused. Everything is all jumbled in your head, and you have to work it out until it makes sense."

Meg shook her head in denial.

A gentle breeze touched her brow, feather soft. "Sometimes it helps to write about your feelings."

"I don't have anyone to write to."

"You can write to me. I'll keep your secrets."

Meg thought about it for a moment, then came to a decision. It would be nice to have someone to talk to. "Okay. What's your name?"

"Gemma. My name is Gemma."

****

The next day Meg opened a brand-new composition book and started writing:

Dear Gemma,

When I told Mrs. Shay I wanted to write about my feelings, she said that was a good idea and gave me this brand new notebook. I've never had anything new before and it's all mine...

Before Meg could finish, a skinny girl with skinned knees and red hair plopped down beside her. Meg slammed the book shut.

"I'm Lucy," she said. "Want to be friends?"

Meg was shocked by the girl's openness, but her smile was contagious. "Okay. But you can't read my diary. It's private."

Lucy tipped her head to the side, as if considering it, then her face brightened with a smile. "Okay. Deal."

Lucy pointed to a bruise on Meg's arm. "What happened?"

Meg tugged on her shirt, trying to cover the deep-purple bruise. "I fell," she said.

Lucy lowered her eyes and frowned, then nodded her head. "Yeah, I fall sometimes, too."

They held each other's gaze for a long moment. Meg knew that Lucy understood. Everything that needed to be said remained unspoken, but a friendship was forged from the silence.

"Come on," Lucy said. "I'll show you where the game room is."

Chapter Five

Present Day

When the phone rang, Ben jerked awake, flailing half on and half off the couch. His first thought was of Meg. He reached for the phone in a sleep-blinded fog, but only managed to sweep it off the coffee table. He stumbled to his knees and grabbed the phone off the floor. "Hello? Lucy?"

"No, pal. It's me, Josh."

Ben exhaled a deep breath, waiting for his heartbeat to return to normal.

"You okay, Ben?"

"Yeah. I just sat up too quickly. What time is it?"

"Almost nine."

"In the morning?" Ben rubbed his face. "I have to get back to the hospital."

"That's why I'm calling," Josh said. "We just, we're all thinking about you and, you know, take as much time as you need."

"As much time? God, I hadn't even thought about work."

"I know, buddy. That's what I'm saying. You take care of Meg and don't worry about work." He cleared his throat. "How's she doing?"

"It's hard to say. The doctors put her in a coma to ease the swelling in her brain. We won't know much until they bring her out of it. Even then..." His voice cracked. He didn't want to think about what might lie ahead. Meg was alive. That was all that mattered.

"Well," Josh said, "Max Reed is covering for you until you get back, so that's one thing less for you to worry about."

Ben raked his fingers through his hair.

"Thanks," he said. "I'll...uh...get back to you as soon as I know something concrete."

He hung up the phone, knowing that he'd have to face going back to work sooner or later, if only for the paycheck. It wasn't as if he hated his job. The students were bright, enthusiastic, and talented. But Ben learned the hard way that talent wasn't enough. He'd seen many talented writers tossed by the wayside with broken hearts and shattered dreams.

Hell, he was a classic case. His first book had garnered rave reviews, climbed the bestseller lists, and turned him into an overnight success. Then came the rejections, the doubts and fears. Maybe it was all a fluke? Maybe he didn't have another great book in him? Eventually, he'd stopped trying. Fewer and fewer people asked when his next book was coming out.

Truth was, there was no second book. Living with Meg's constant depression left little time or energy for dreaming. Finally, he'd given in and taken a job teaching a creative writing course at the local community college.

Maybe it was true what they say—*those who can't, teach.*

Pushing aside his own feelings of failure, Ben called Lucy's cell phone. As expected, there had been no change in Meg's condition during the night.

"Take your time," Lucy said. "I don't have to leave until noon, so why don't you get some things taken care of at home and come back then."

Ben started to argue, but Lucy was right. He wouldn't be any good to Meg when she came out of the coma if he didn't take care of himself now.

****

She is a rock. She has no feelings, no thoughts, no dreams. There are no words, only this moment. She is still, smooth and silent, warmed by the sun and kissed by the breeze. She has no name and cannot move. A rock can't be hurt. A rock can't be blamed. A rock simply is.

****

Ben put a load of laundry in the washer and made his first cup of coffee before turning on the computer. The act was more habit than anything else. He stared at the screen with no idea of what to write. It had been that way for longer than he cared to admit. He wouldn't call it writer's block. More like writer's apathy. He couldn't force himself to care about fictional characters. Especially now.

After ten minutes or so, he stood and stretched his back. The blank screen stared back, hiding its secrets. He made his way to the kitchen and poured a second cup of coffee, inhaling the aroma deep into his lungs. Coffee was his drug of choice. Meg preferred English tea. It was only one of the many ways they differed.

Ben opened the refrigerator and stared inside, but nothing appealed to him. After a few minutes, he gave up searching, closed the refrigerator, and put everything back where it belonged. The kitchen was as neat and orderly as a factory showroom. Organization was one of Meg's little quirks. For someone whose mind was in constant chaos, Meg's surroundings were impeccable. Maybe it was the one thing she felt she had control over.

Coffee cup in hand, he made his way to the computer and sat staring at the blank screen. He had notes somewhere—ideas jotted down before going to sleep, thoughts for a new book. He wasn't sure where they were and didn't really care. Sitting at the computer was his form of punishment, like ritual flagellation. How much could he hurt himself by sitting here unable to do the one thing he once loved?

Screw it.

Ben turned the computer off with a sigh of resignation. Resisting the urge to call the hospital to check in with Lucy again, he plopped himself down in front of the TV and searched for the remote. It wasn't on the coffee table or the end table. He reached down between the cushions where it sometimes disappeared and brushed against something.

It wasn't the remote, however. What he'd found was Meg's journal. He'd seen her writing in it hundreds of times. He'd never asked to read it, and she'd never said he couldn't. It was simply understood. This was her sacred space. Reading it now would be an invasion of her privacy, no matter how tempting.

He ran his fingers over the cover. It was a simple, department-store notebook covered in bright pink and yellow daisies, like something a little girl would choose for her first day of school. What if he opened it only to discover that Meg *had* in fact been suicidal? What if their argument was the final straw that had pushed her over the edge? How could he live with the guilt?

He tucked the journal back between the seat cushions for Meg to find when she came home, then checked his watch. He'd promised Lucy he wouldn't come back to relieve her until noon. It was almost eleven.

Close enough.

Chapter Six

It was hard to tell who was more embarrassed when Ben slipped into the hospital room and caught Lucy reading his book. She tried to hide it at first, then shrugged. "I'm trying to figure out what she sees in you."

"Gee, thanks."

"I didn't mean it like that. I've known Meg all my life. She's always been attracted to the wrong kind of men. She has a weakness for bad boys. Edgy. Dangerous. The more dangerous, the better." She glanced at Meg, then back again. "Maybe she's always had a death wish."

Ben wasn't sure how to respond to that.

"Then you came along," Lucy said. "Thoughtful and sensitive. The brooding artist. Not her type at all. Unless she saw something in you the rest of us didn't." She held up the book. "I thought maybe if I read this, I'd see some of that bad boy lurking beneath the surface."

"Nope. Sorry to disappoint you. Nothing lurking below the surface here."

Nothing except failure.

"You're not a bad writer," Lucy said.

Ben rolled his eyes. "Oh please, you'll make my head swell."

"Sarcasm. That's a good start. Maybe Meg saw

that as potential."

"Or maybe she realized there was nothing wrong with falling in love with a nice guy for a change."

Lucy shot him a tolerant smile but didn't respond. She tucked the book into her tote bag and stood. "I'll be back tomorrow morning so you can go to work."

"I have a substitute. I can stay with Meg."

"It's going to be a long wait. The doctor said she may need weeks to heal." Lucy's eyes were red and swollen, but she forced a brave face. "No sense in both of us sitting here waiting for her to wake up." Her expression softened sympathetically. "Go home tonight and sleep, then get back into your normal work routine. The doctor will let us know when they're ready to wake her up."

As much as he hated to admit it, Ben knew she was right.

When Lucy left, Ben pulled the chair up close to Meg's bedside. He reached for her hand, which was cool and unresponsive. It was hard to see her this way, with tubes strapped to her face, wires and monitors and drips attached to her body. There was no way to pull her into his arms and hold her close, no way to ease her pain.

He straightened the sheet over her, resting his hand on her chest to feel the gentle breath, the barely perceptible rise and fall. If only he could find a way to keep her peaceful and untroubled when she regained consciousness.

****

A white cloth on a white table. On the table is a book. She rushes forward, convinced the book holds the secret of everything. She opens it only to discover the first page is totally blank. And the next. And the next. She flips the pages faster and faster, hoping the story will begin, but there is no beginning, no middle, no end. Only emptiness. Page after page. Day after day. She knows there's more to this book. The empty pages are ripe with possibility. A clean slate waiting to be imprinted with a brand new story.

****

When the night nurse tried to send him home, Ben's first reaction was to argue. But suddenly he was hungry, not so much for food but company. He needed to be someplace where death and dying wasn't a way of life. And he knew just the place.

It was a short drive to Cappie's Sports Bar, which had the best Reuben sandwiches in town, ice-cold beer, and dozens of monitors covering every sport imaginable.

It was also where he'd first met Meg.

He took a seat at the same booth where he'd spotted her almost five years ago. She'd been working her way through college, going to classes during the day and bartending at Cappie's in the evening. He'd noticed her carrying a tray of drinks across the room, wearing a tight black skirt that only seemed short because her legs were so damned long. A crisp white shirt set off hair the color of molten chocolate, which was pulled back into a flirty ponytail.

He'd wanted her then and there. He still did, but lately lust had been tempered by aggravation.

"Hey, handsome," she'd said in a voice that rolled like satin over his skin. "What can I get you?"

He was one hundred percent certain she called all of her customers handsome, but that didn't stop him from sitting taller and giving her his broadest smile. "I'll have a Reuben and whatever you have on tap."

"Bud, Bud Light, Miller..."

"Make it a Bud." The beer no longer mattered. One look in her eyes and he was a goner. She shot him a quick little half smile and walked away with his order, hips swaying seductively in that little black skirt.

Ben smiled at the memory. No one would have called Meg beautiful, but in a room full of beautiful women, all eyes were drawn to her—to the shine of her dark brown hair, the signature red lipstick she always wore framing a movie-star smile, to the single teardrop pendant resting provocatively at the dip of her cleavage, drawing the eye to what she unashamedly referred to as her best features.

When she'd returned with the check after he'd finished eating, her phone number was scribbled on the back. He'd called her the next day, and they'd been together ever since.

A hand on his shoulder startled him from those long-ago memories. He turned and gasped. For a moment he'd thought...

"I'm sorry, Professor Jackson," the girl said. "I saw you sitting here alone and..."

Ben stood, recognizing the girl from one of his classes, although he couldn't place her name. "It's okay. For a moment, you reminded me of my wife." And she did, in an eerie way. She was a tad shorter than Meg, and her hair a bit lighter. But their features were uncannily similar.

"I heard what happened," she said. "The accident, I mean. I just wanted to say I'm sorry and I hope everything works out okay."

"Thanks," he said. *Sierra*. He remembered now. "Thanks, Sierra." Odd how he hadn't noticed before how much she looked like Meg. They could have been sisters. Maybe because he was here at Cappie's, surrounded by memories of Meg when she was about the same age as Sierra.

"May I?" she asked, gesturing to the empty seat at the table.

And there it was. The difference between the two. Meg wouldn't have asked. She'd have sat down with a wink, rested her elbows on the table and leaned forward to capture his every word as if no one else existed.

Sierra lowered her eyes. "I loved your book," she said with a shy smile. "I couldn't put it down. Honestly, I stayed up all night to finish it."

"Oh. Thanks. You realize that reading my book isn't part of the curriculum."

"I know," she said. "But when I heard you were teaching this course, I just had to read it for myself. I wasn't disappointed."

"Thanks, that's exactly what I was going for."

Color rushed to her face. "I didn't mean…"

"I know. I'm just a little sensitive right now." He certainly wasn't going to discuss his writing problems with a stranger—and a student, no less.

"So, I was wondering…"

Oh, here it comes. He cringed waiting for the question he'd heard a thousand times and didn't have an answer for. *When's your next book coming out?*

"I was wondering," she said, lowering her eyes. "I was wondering if maybe you'd sign it for me. If I bring it to class one day?"

Ben hadn't expected that. He was secretly

delighted. However, it made him feel like an even bigger fraud.

"I mean, if it's not too much trouble."

"No trouble at all."

"Okay, then." She stood to leave. "I'll see you in class."

He nodded.

"Oh, and one more thing." She reached into her purse and pulled out a piece of paper. "Some of us put together a play for the drama club, and we'd love your opinion...as a professional, that is. It's a few weeks away, but if you're available we'd love you to come."

Ben folded the flyer and tucked it into his pocket. "Maybe," he said. "I'll see what I can do."

"I'm playing the lead," she said, eyes lighting with excitement.

"Oh? You're an actress, too?"

"Acting is my passion. I hope to act, write and direct one day."

Ben couldn't help but smile. Her enthusiasm was infectious. He'd forgotten what it was like to be that young and hopeful, to pursue your passion with no idea of the bumps in the road ahead. "I'm sure you'll be great."

"Thanks," she said. "I hope to see you there." With that she turned and joined her friends across the room.

Ben felt older than his thirty years and infinitely wiser. Maybe he would stop by and see the play. It wouldn't hurt to escape the pain for a few hours.

The thought was followed by an immediate pang of guilt. He had no right to even consider enjoying an evening out when Meg lay fighting for her life.

Chapter Seven

Over the next few weeks, Ben and Lucy fell into a regular routine. Ben went to work in the morning and Lucy sat with Meg during the day. After a quick stop for fast food, he'd head to the hospital and trade places with Lucy. Sometimes they'd chat for a little while, but lately it seemed Lucy couldn't wait to escape. He knew how she felt. It had been weeks now. There were only so many things you could talk about to an unconscious patient, only so many crossword puzzles you could do, and only so many prayers you could say.

The truth was, he couldn't stand seeing Meg this way. It was getting harder to remember how alive she once was. Her hair had lost its shine, her skin no longer glowed with health, and he barely remembered her smile. The longer she stayed like this, the harder it was to imagine her actually coming out of the coma.

Lately the classroom had become his haven, the hospital room his hell. He wasn't sure how much longer he could sit by his wife's hospital bed listening to her breathing and wondering if she'd ever open her eyes again. His life had become a constant struggle between hope and despair.

The sound of laughter jarred him from his thoughts and brought him back to the classroom.

Sierra was standing at her desk, reading her short story to the class from a clutch of typed sheets:

"It was terrible. She pushed her way to the front row seat so we could have the best view. So when a camel made a break for it..."

Her date's eyes widened. "You mean she...?"

"Yes, my mother was killed by a runaway camel at the circus."

"I'm sorry." He pressed his lips into a tight line, but a snort escaped, sounding like the last gasp of a drowning boar.

"So were the circus owners," she replied. "But that didn't stop us from suing them."

"Ah..."

"And that's how I became the proud owner of Lydia Jean's Camel-Free Circus and All-Male Review."

"I'm not sure how the two are connected," he said, no longer trying to hide the smile on his face.

Ben listened to the rest of the story, delighted by Sierra's quirky sense of humor. By the time she finished reading, the entire class was smiling along with him. To be honest, Ben couldn't remember the last time he'd felt a genuine smile, not one pasted on for polite society. It felt good.

"Very nice, Sierra," he said with a nod. "You have a great sense of humor that comes through in your writing. The pacing was great and the dialogue sounded completely natural."

A blush of pink colored to her cheeks. "Thank you. I practiced reading aloud as you suggested. It really helped."

Ben was too jaded to be flattered. He'd become accustomed to eager students waiting for the local celebrity to share the secrets they were sure he knew—

the secret of writing a bestselling novel, the secret road to fame and fortune. If he knew, would he be standing in front of them teaching?

They couldn't wait to read for him. They wanted approval, needed validation. Well hell, don't we all?

He wanted to tell them that talent was cheap. Hundreds of talented people fell by the wayside every day. But that's not what they paid him for. He was here to teach them the craft of writing. That's all that could be taught.

Sierra was waiting for him when class let out. Instead of finding an excuse to blow her off, however, Ben nodded and smiled.

She fell into step beside him, taking three clipped steps to every two of his. "I hope you don't mind," she said. "I wanted a moment to talk to you."

"I really enjoyed your story," he said.

"Thank you. It means a lot to me."

"Me too," he said. "It's the first good laugh I've had since…"

She cleared her throat. "I'm sure it hasn't been easy." She looked at him, then away again. "That's why I wanted to talk to you. Remember the play I told you about? The one I co-wrote?"

Ben shook his head, then reached forward and held the door open as they left the building, surprised at how the bright afternoon sun turned the campus lawn a sharp, vibrant green. "I'm sorry. I totally forgot."

"That's understandable considering all you have on your mind. That's why I wanted to remind you. The play is Saturday night." She barely paused for breath as they made their way toward the parking lot. "I mean if you're available. It would mean a lot to me."

It might have been the angle of the afternoon sunlight or the bend in the path, but Ben noticed their silhouettes looked closer than they actually were. Feeling a twinge of discomfort, he took a step to the side, putting distance between their shadows.

Ben stopped when they reached his car. Every instinct urged him to say no. His life revolved around the classroom and his wife's hospital bed. But her face was so hopeful. And it had felt good to forget for a few moments today. What would it hurt?

"Sure," he said. "I'll make arrangements at the hospital for Saturday night. What time is the play?"

"Seven." She clutched her books to her chest. "I'll see you then." She turned and practically skipped away. Ben smiled. There was probably less than ten years age difference between them, but he felt decades older.

Inside the car, he turned on the ignition and the radio came on. The strains of a familiar tune clutched his heart. It was their song—his and Meg's. Memories flooded over him, bringing with them a slew of emotions—love, lust and longing.

He switched the radio off and took a deep breath. There were other memories there as well. Nights when Meg didn't come home. Days when she kept secrets close to her chest. Meg had many secrets. Ben didn't pry because he was afraid of losing her. Walls went up quick and took forever to tear down again.

Ben sat in the parking lot watching people gathered in groups or walking with a sense of purpose to their next destination. He felt as though the world was revolving around him. His life was stagnant and still.

Before he could change his mind, Ben reached for his phone and punched in Lucy's number. "Hey," he said when she answered. "I'm leaving now. Want me to pick up something to eat on the way?"

"No thanks," she replied. "I have dinner plans for tonight."

Dinner plans. Even Lucy had a life outside of the hospital. That only confirmed his decision. "Okay. Listen, I was wondering if you'd mind switching shifts with me Saturday? Some of the students here are putting on a play and asked me if I'd come. Since it's Saturday, I can stay at the hospital during the day if you can cover at night."

"Sure. No problem. I wanted to get some shopping done anyway. Perfect timing."

Ben hung up and drove home, surprised to find himself looking forward to an evening out.

****

Saturday morning Ben rose early, tucked the papers he hadn't finished grading the night before into his briefcase and left for the hospital.

One of Meg's nurses stopped him on the way to her room. "Oh, Mr. Tyler. I was just about to call you."

"Why? What's wrong?"

"Nothing. Nothing's wrong. Dr. Beckett asked if I could set up a meeting today with you. Will you be available this afternoon? About 2:00?"

Ben exhaled a sigh of relief. "I'll be right here all day." Wasn't that a husband's job? To sit with his comatose wife every minute of the day and night? Meg was his responsibility. He shouldn't depend so much on Lucy or the nurses to be here. Maybe he should skip the play after all.

Ben made his way to Meg's bedside. She looked thinner than he remembered. She was so pale he could see the trail of blue veins beneath her skin—a swirl of ink on faded papyrus.

"Don't go," he whispered, brushing the hair from her forehead. "Stay with us, Meg." He waited, but there was no response. He wondered if there ever would be or if Meg would stay this way forever.

For better and for worse. In sickness and in health.

Vows made without really considering their impact. They were just words until something happened and you realized that the vows you made are real and can change the rest of your life. Forever.

He pulled up a chair beside Meg's bed, opened his briefcase and took out the assignments that still needed to be graded.

"You're going to like this one, Meg. It's written by a boy named Jason who wears skin-tight pants, flannel shirts and no socks. Doesn't seem to hurt him with the girls. He's got that brooding poet lumberjack look going on. Talented, but so in love with his words that he forgets he's supposed to tell a story."

He read the assignments to Meg, one after the other, wondering what, if anything, registered. Could she even hear him? Did she recognize his voice? His touch?

He shook his head and moved on to the next assignment. This was Sierra's story. "You'd like her, Meg. She reminds me of you. She could be your younger sister."

****

Meg dreams in colors she can taste, words sprout wings and take flight. She tries to read the story they write but the words dip and swirl in meaningless metaphors. In total silence, letters fly against a wide,

38

wide sky.

Y-Y-Y-y-y-wy-wy-why-WHY-WHY?

She closes her eyes, blotting out all the questions. She has no answers.

****

Ben graded the last paper just as Dr. Beckett entered the room. He stood, clutching the papers to his chest. "How's she doing?"

"She's doing very well," the doctor said, glancing from Meg to the chart in her hands. "So well, in fact, that we're going to start weaning her off the medications."

Ben was encouraged by the compassion in her eyes. "You mean you're taking her out of the coma?"

The doctor nodded. "The swelling is down, and she seems to be healing nicely. If we take her off the medications, she should regain consciousness naturally."

Ben exhaled. "Thank God." He stepped close to the bed and lifted Meg's hand. It was cool and lifeless. But it wouldn't be for long. "How soon before she wakes up?"

"We've already started reducing her medication. It'll be a few days before it's out of her system completely."

"So Monday?"

"Yes. I wanted you to know so you could be here if...*when* she regains consciousness."

Ben pretended not to notice the slip. Of course Meg would regain consciousness. She'd wake up as good as new and they'd go back to the way things used to be.

"I'll tell Lucy," he said. "She'll want to be here

when Meg wakes up too."

Dr. Beckett nodded, then turned to leave. "I'll see you Monday."

"We'll be here."

When the doctor left the room, Ben clasped Meg's hand. "Did you hear that, Meg? Everything's going to be okay. You're coming back to us soon."

That was exactly what he told Lucy when she came to relieve him. The two of them celebrated with cafeteria coffee, promising to bring champagne on Monday.

"We'll have a real celebration then, won't we Ben?"

Her smile was contagious. "We will. Yes, we will."

Chapter Eight

Twenty Years Ago - St. Ophelia's Home for Girls

Dear Gemma,

I don't hate it here. The food is okay. At least it's hot. I don't make a lot of friends. Most of the girls only stay a little while, anyway. Then they leave. Either they go back home or get adopted or whatever. No sense getting close to someone who's only going to leave, right?

Except Lucy. She and I seem to be permanent fixtures here. Nobody wants either of us. Guess you could say we're friends, but I'm waiting for the day she leaves me, too.

Me? I guess I'll be here forever. Like I said, it's not so bad. I don't hate it here.

Love,

Megan

Meg and Lucy loved playing dominoes. They'd play for hours on the scarred game room table. They didn't care who won or lost. One game followed another as they talked, and laughed, and dreamed their little-girl dreams.

They weren't supposed to take things out of the game room, but even more than playing dominoes, Lucy and Meg loved building domino trails, around the stalls and sink, making loops and swirls and bridges over toilet paper rolls, until they ran out of domino tiles to place. When an accidental nudge sent the entire design clicking and clattering over the tiled floor like old bones, *clackity clack clack*, they'd collapse in laughter, holding their bellies until the laughter stopped for a moment, only to start up all over again.

Meg heard footsteps outside the door and held a finger over her lips to try to hold back the giggles. She gave a guilty start when the bathroom door opened. Mrs. Shay stood in the doorway, hands on her hips, looking stern. "What are you girls doing in here?"

Lucy jumped to her feet, shuffled one foot in front of the other and batted her eyes innocently. "Just playing dominoes, Mrs. Shay. They don't fall good on the rug in the game room."

One side of Mrs. Shay's mouth quirked up, then back again, as if a smile was trying to escape. "Well, you know the rules." She crinkled her nose. "And this is no place to play. Pick them up for now and get ready for dinner. Wash your hands first."

"Yes, ma'am," they said in unison.

Mrs. Shay turned to Meg and a shadow crossed her face, gone as quickly as it appeared. "Megan, could you come into my office while Lucy picks up here?"

Meg glanced at Lucy, who shrugged her shoulders. She couldn't think of any reason to be called into Mrs. Shay's office. Maybe it was about the cookies she'd sneaked out of the kitchen yesterday. Or maybe her mom and dad had come to take her home?

Meg followed Mrs. Shay down a long hallway and into the corner room that served as her office. It always smelled nice in here, she thought. Like peppermint candy. She sat on one side of the desk as Mrs. Shay settled on the other. Meg noticed fresh flowers in a glass and a framed photo on the desk of two little girls in pastel Easter bonnets. She hadn't thought of Mrs. Shay as having a life outside of St. Ophelia's. For some reason, the thought stirred a strange yearning inside. What would it be like to wake up in the morning with parents who dressed you in pretty bonnets then proudly displayed your picture on their desk?

Meg glanced from the picture to Mrs. Shay and back again. She imagined Mrs. Shay wearing an apron and cooking with her pretty blonde hair pulled back in a ponytail while the girls colored at the table. Maybe the girls would tease each other and get silly, then Mrs. Shay would scold them and say, "Now girls, you know the rules. Put those crayons away and get ready for dinner." Then that smile that had been hiding would light up her face, and the girls would scurry off with a "Yes, Momma," all glowing cheeks and bouncy curls.

Meg sighed.

Mrs. Shay cleared her throat. "Megan, I'm afraid I have some bad news for you."

Meg didn't like the look on Mrs. Shay's face, so she looked away. She focused instead on a fancy pin on her collar. It was a dragonfly with jeweled wings. She couldn't take her eyes off it, not even when Mrs. Shay told her that her parents weren't coming back. They'd moved away leaving no forwarding address. No one knew where they'd gone.

Mrs. Shay insisted St. Ophelia's was doing everything they could to locate them. Meg nodded, never taking her gaze off the dragonfly pin. Her eyes watered, making the wings shimmer. They almost seemed to flutter, and Meg was sure the dragonfly would lift off Mrs. Shay's collar and fly away. Fly far away, someplace where kids were loved, and people didn't leave them behind like a piece of trash.

Mrs. Shay came around the desk and leaned over. She put her arms around Meg and held her close. "It'll be all right. I promise."

Meg didn't think it would ever be all right, but she leaned into Mrs. Shay's arms. The hug felt soft, comforting, and safe. Maybe this was what a mother's embrace was supposed to feel like. She felt a sudden pang of jealousy for the girls in the picture frame who took it for granted.

A sob escaped Meg's throat. She pulled in a deep breath and straightened her spine. She wouldn't cry. Crying got you nowhere. She pulled away from Mrs. Shay. She didn't deserve to be hugged, to be loved, to be wanted.

As she jerked to her feet, the dragonfly pin pulled loose from Mrs. Shay's collar and fell to the floor. Meg leaned over and picked it up, cradling it in her palm. So pretty. It seemed to represent all the things she could never have. She closed her hand around the dragonfly and felt a flash of pain as the pin pricked the pad of her thumb.

And just like that, the dam burst, and she couldn't hold back her tears any longer. She cried and cried as Mrs. Shay rocked her back and forth. When the tears stopped, she felt drained. Drained and empty and weak. She wiped her nose with the tissue Mrs. Shay handed her, and vowed then and there never to feel weak again.

She tried to hand the dragonfly back, but Mrs. Shay shook her head. "You keep it, honey.

Meg shook her head. "No, I..." She didn't deserve

pretty things. She'd stolen a cookie and even her parents didn't want her.

"Take it," Mrs. Shay said, her eyes filled with kindness. "Let it remind you that you have the power within you to transform your life. One day you'll fly free and become anything you want to be."

Meg held the dragonfly close to her heart. She wanted to believe Mrs. Shay. Maybe it was true. Maybe not. But at least it gave her a reason to hope.

Chapter Nine

Present Day

Ben wasn't sure his mood could get any better. He settled into his seat and opened the playbill, surprised by a twinge of pride seeing Sierra's name listed as co-writer. After all, she *was* his student.

The curtain opened, and the actors came on stage. From the first word uttered, Ben recognized Sierra's writing and quirky sense of humor. He was surprised to see she even played a minor character in the opening scene.

The play chronicled the adventures of a nerdy but likeable scientist, Professor Willymeier, who discovers a way to go back in time. Instead of publishing his findings, however, he uses the knowledge to change events from his past, those that he believed kept him from being successful and catching the eye of the girl he had a crush on in high school.

Unfortunately, nothing works as planned. Each return trip leaves Professor Willymeier in worse shape than before, and each time he returns he shouts, "No, no, no! This is *not* my story!"

For someone who grew up reading Ray Bradbury and Harlan Ellison, this science fiction spoof was right up Ben's alley. By the end of the play, the character had found the girl but lost the ability to invent the time travel device in the first place, and Ben had a stitch in his side from laughing so hard. He stood and cheered, along with the rest of the audience.

Only when the curtain closed for the final time did Ben feel a twinge of guilt for enjoying himself while Meg was still lying in a coma. Not for long, though, he told himself. Soon she'd be back to normal, and the two of them would enjoy evenings like this together.

Ben made his way to the stage door. Sierra had promised to leave him a backstage pass. He gave his name to the security guard and was ushered through a hallway and up a flight of stairs to the stage.

Sierra met him halfway, her face flushed with excitement. "Did you like it?"

"I did," he assured her. "I laughed more than I've laughed in a long, long time."

Sierra grasped Ben's arm and pulled him over to meet some of the actors on the stage, crediting him with everything she'd learned about writing.

"No, no," Ben said. "I can only take credit for teaching the craft. Sierra has a natural talent for writing that can't be taught."

"Thank you," she said, lowering her eyes. When she looked up again, they glistened. "Would you like to join us? We're going out for drinks to celebrate."

Ben was tempted but declined. "No, I think I'm going to run back to the hospital for a few hours." The truth was, he couldn't shake the feeling of guilt for enjoying himself as much as he had. If felt like a betrayal.

"Oh, okay, but..." Sierra rushed back to a table and picked up a copy of his book. "Could you sign this for me before you go?"

Ben swallowed hard over a lump in his throat. It had been a long time since someone had asked him to sign a copy of his book. He was secretly delighted, but at the same time it made him feel like even more of a fraud. *Imposter Syndrome*—he'd read about it in psychology books. Reading about it was one thing, but living it was another. "Sure," he said. "On one condition."

"What's that?"

He handed Sierra the playbill. "If you'll sign this for me."

Color rushed to her cheeks. "Really?"

"Of course." He reached into his pocket and handed her a pen.

She signed her name on the cover, then smiled at him, her eyes wide with what could only be perceived as hero worship. Ben was immediately drawn back to the days when Meg would look at him in the same exact way. How long had it been? When had he stopped being her hero?

It had been a long time since Meg had looked at him with anything but anger. He wasn't even sure why she was angry most of the time. Sometimes he thought if she rolled her eyes at him one more time they'd roll right out of their sockets.

Ben closed his eyes and shook his head. He shouldn't think about Meg that way. Not now when she was trapped in her head and unaware. They'd work out their issues once this was all over.

He quickly signed the book and handed it back to Sierra, the glow of the evening rapidly fading. "Thanks for inviting me," he said. "I really enjoyed it." With that, he turned and left the stage.

****

Ben walked through the darkened parking lot with long, determined strides, leaving the light and laughter behind him. Back to reality.

He drove to the hospital, but when he reached the entrance, he almost kept going. Visiting hours were over and no one was expecting him tonight. Meg wouldn't even know he was there.

At the last minute he parked and went inside.

"Hey, Mr. Tyler. You're here late." It was Janie Black, one of his favorite nurses.

"I was out for the evening and decided to stop in."

She offered him a sympathetic smile. "I hear Monday's going to be a big day. I'll be praying for you both."

"Thanks, Janie. We can use all the prayers we can get." He gestured toward the corridor leading to Meg's room. "You don't mind if I sneak in after visiting hours, do you?"

"No, we've already broken the rules once tonight. Meg's brother came by and asked to see her."

"Brother?"

"Yes. He's probably still in there now. Want me to check?"

"No. I'll do it myself." Ben rushed down the corridor toward Meg's room with one thought on his mind.

Meg didn't have a brother.

Halfway down the hall, Ben saw a man he didn't recognize leaving Meg's room. "Hey. Stop!"

The man turned, studying Ben with eyes as hard and brittle as weathered slate.

"Who are you?" Ben asked.

"Nobody," the man said, avoiding Ben's gaze. "I have the wrong room, that's all."

"Did you tell the nurse you were Meg's brother?"

"Nope. She must have misunderstood. I was looking for someone else."

Ben had studied body language to research character traits for his books, so he knew the man was lying.

They stared at each other for a long moment until finally the cocky, James Dean lookalike shrugged and turned to leave. Ben committed the man's features to memory. If he was someone close to Meg, Lucy would know.

He turned and stepped inside Meg's room. She lay in exactly the same position she'd been when he left. Her hair had been washed, brushed, and twisted into a side ponytail. Ben was tempted to let her hair loose and run his fingers through it.

The first thing he'd noticed about Meg was her hair. It had been long, lush, and pulled back into a sexy, swingy ponytail, so when she walked with that rolling-hip gait, her hair swung back and forth seductively. It was hypnotizing. He'd wanted to run his finger through the long waves, wrap it around his wrist, and let it fall loose and sexy.

Later he'd fallen in love with her smile, her self-deprecating humor, and her razor-sharp wit. But it was her hair that first seduced him.

Careful not to dislodge the intravenous tubes, he lifted Meg's hand and brushed his lips across her fingers. "Hey babe. Let me tell you about the play I saw tonight. I really didn't have high hopes for it, to be honest, based on past experiences. Student plays can sometimes be tedious and pretentious affairs."

He stopped and took a breath. "Not this one, however. It was clever and charming. Thought provoking. Remind me to take you to see it when we spring you out of this place, okay? You can wear that cute little black dress you bought for my parents' anniversary party. And that necklace you were eyeing at the jewelry store? Well, I think I might just surprise you with it."

He breathed in a deep sigh. "Things are going to be different, Meg. I promise."

****

Meg dreams of falling snow drifting across a field. Up ahead she sees the same wrought-iron gate she'd seen before, glazed with ice and frosted with snow. A movement catches her eye. A dragonfly, glittering in the sun, its shadow gliding over the snow. It dances and swirls, as if imploring her to follow. And so she does, until she reaches the gate and stops.

The dragonfly hovers on the other side, its iridescent wings leaving stained-glass patterns on the white, white snow. It lands on the gate, making a sound on the ice like tiny crystal bells.

She touches the gate, but the snow is too deep, resisting any movement. A voice whispers in her ear. "Push it open."

She turns and sees a woman standing beside her. For a moment, the woman seems to have wings like the dragonfly, but when she blinks, they're gone. It's just an ordinary woman who looks vaguely familiar. "I'm so happy to see you," the woman says with a genuine smile.

"Who are you?"

The woman tips her head. "You know me. You've always known me. I'm Gemma."

The name is familiar. Gemma points toward the gate. "Go ahead. Open it."

"No," Meg says, suddenly afraid of what's on the other side. The snow is deep, buried secrets lurking beneath the surface. Secrets she doesn't want to uncover. Let them stay buried beneath the cold blanket of snow. "I can't."

She turns away from the gate and walks through the snowy field. Gemma stays by her side, in silent communion. She turns. "What do you want?"

Gemma tips her head knowingly. A flurry of snow swirls around her like a cloak. "You should think about waking up," she says.

"No." The fear is too great, the sadness too deep. "Not yet."

Gemma nods, then turns away. "When you're ready, come find me."

She turns away, then back again. But Gemma is gone and when Meg looks back there's only one set of footprints in the snow.

Chapter Ten

Ben arrived at the hospital bright and early Monday morning. He found Lucy already settled in the hospital waiting room. She held up her coffee cup in a salute. Ben nodded, poured himself a cup from the hospitality pot set up in the corner, then joined her on the faux leather couch. "Has the doctor been in yet?"

"Haven't seen her."

They sipped their coffee in silence, each lost in their own thoughts.

"Tell me about the orphanage where you and Meg met," Ben said, desperate to learn more about his wife's secret past.

Lucy frowned and took a slow, thoughtful sip of her coffee. "It wasn't really an orphanage. St. Ophelia's was a home for girls whose families couldn't take care of them for one reason or another. We weren't orphans in the strictest sense. We had families. Some were in jail or on drugs or incapable of taking care of us for one reason or another. It might have been better if we didn't. Then we might have been adopted and given a chance for a better life."

Lucy leaned back, her gaze far away, as if looking into the past. "Three times Meg went back to live with her parents, and three times she returned to St. Ophelia's, her light a little dimmer, her smile more forced, her spirit a little more broken. She wouldn't talk about what happened when she was away, but I knew it was bad. I could read the unspoken message in the bruises on her body, the terror lurking silently behind her eyes."

Lucy gave Ben a quivering smile. "I don't know how the system works. I believe there are people who really care and want to do the right thing. But sometimes the right thing is the wrong thing and sometimes strangers are kinder than the people who are supposed to protect you."

She pursed her lips and frowned. "I do know that each time Meg came back, I was happy. Happy to have my friend back. Happy to no longer be alone in that place." She gave Ben a sad smile. "What does that make me?"

Ben squeezed her shoulder. "It makes you human."

Lucy closed her eyes and took a deep breath. "Meg was—*is*—my best friend." She rolled up her sleeve, revealing a faint, jagged scar at her wrist.

At Ben's horrified gasp, she shook her head. "No, it's not what it seems. Meg had this pin—a butterfly or dragonfly or some winged something. I think she found it, because I seem to remember one of the ladies in the office wearing it all the time. Anyway, we used the pin to scratch at our skin until it bled. Then we rubbed our wrists together and pronounced ourselves blood sisters."

Her voice softened and became child-like. *"When we're apart and when we're together, we'll always remain blood sisters forever."* She shrugged and smiled. "Meg wrote the line and made me memorize it for days before we performed the ceremony."

Ben could almost see those two lost little girls

holding on to each other for survival. He wished he could snatch them up and tell them not to worry, that everything was going to be all right.

Or was it? Maybe too much damage had been done and nothing would ever be the same.

Lucy traced the scar on her wrist, still lost in the past. "We were all the family we needed. And it was sweeter because we chose each other. It didn't matter if no one else wanted us. We had each other." She looked up, her eyes soft with unshed tears. "Forever."

They sat in comfortable silence, each lost in their own thoughts. When Dr. Beckett passed by, she nodded at them as she headed toward Meg's room. They both leaned forward expectantly, even though they knew the procedure to bring Meg fully awake would take a while.

It broke Ben's heart to hear how Meg had gone from a happy, carefree little girl to the broken woman she'd become. And yet... "I don't understand," he said. "The past is behind her now. She has everything she ever wanted—a home, a family, a job she loves. Why does she still battle with depression?"

Lucy shrugged. "Maybe it's not the big things that wear us down, but a lifetime of small disappointments, resentment, anger, and abandonment."

"Maybe," Ben said. "God knows, I've tried to make her feel safe and loved, but she pushes me away, hides her real feelings behind a mask of indifference."

"I'm not surprised," Lucy said. "That's what she does. She pushes people away to see if they'll stay. It's a test. If you fail, it only proves that she's right. She's unworthy of being loved." Lucy went on. "She both fears and expects to be abandoned by those she loves. Even after a lifetime of trust and friendship, she still tests me. The difference is, I know the signs and don't let her get away with it."

"You're the one constant in her life," Ben said.

"Not always."

Before Lucy could explain, a nurse poked her head in the waiting room. "Meg is waking up. Dr. Beckett will need a few more minutes with her, then she'll call each of you in."

****

The dragonfly hovers in front of Meg for a moment. She notices blood on the snow. One drop. Two. Then the dragonfly stutters and falls to the ground, frozen and stiff. Its wings grow dim. She reaches down and scoops the lifeless body off the glistening snow. A tear falls and turns to ice—cold, hard, and unfeeling.

She straightens, closing her hand around the lifeless dragonfly and sees a swan glide across the water of a gentle pond. The swan draws closer, leaving a rippling wake behind. As it reaches the edge of the pond, it expands and stands on two legs. The swan transforms into a familiar figure—Gemma. A halo of light surrounds her, like a saint or an angel.

Gemma steps closer, a smile so loving that it makes her heart ache. She's surrounded by unconditional, all-encompassing love. Then Gemma whispers. "It's time to wake up now."

She shakes her head from side to side.

Gentle arms cradle her like a sleeping child. She's rocked, her soul slumbering peacefully. Arms enfold her. Love surrounds her. She is safe and protected. Nothing can reach her. It would be so easy to stay here floating in the void with no worries, no demands.

Gemma caresses her hair lovingly. "I know. But

it's time to wake up. Open your eyes, Meg."

****

"Meg. Open your eyes."

Unable to resist the command, Meg peeked out from beneath swollen lids, then quickly closed them again as the light crept in to assault her eyes. Then slowly, carefully, she opened them wider, a little at a time, until she became accustomed to the light. She saw a woman dressed in white, a tiny sparrow of a woman perhaps in her mid-fifties. Her kind eyes studied Meg beneath a veneer of professionalism.

Meg blinked. "You're not a swan."

"That's correct." Her smile was comforting and warm. "I'm Dr. Beckett."

"Doctor." Meg glanced around the room, taking everything in—the hospital bed, the thin cotton blanket covering her, an I.V. stand, tubes leading to her arms which seemed more slender and delicate than they should be. "Am I sick?"

"You were in an accident."

Meg reached up and felt bandages on her head. "An accident?"

"That's right. Do you remember anything?"

"I remember floating. I remember a swan. No, not a swan. A friend...or an angel." Meg leaned back, suddenly weak from the effort of trying to think.

"Do you remember your name?"

She frowned. It was there, just out of reach. If she thought long enough, hard enough, surely she'd remember her own name. "No," she said with a sigh. "I don't remember anything." Not her name, not who she was, what she did, or why she was here. The only things she remembered were dream images—of dragonflies and snowdrifts and a guardian angel named Gemma. That was the world in which she belonged. Not this room full of strangers, bright lights, and sharp sounds.

The doctor reached out and took her hand. Her touch was warm, her smile comforting. "It's okay. Sometimes this happens after a head trauma. Your name is Meg Tyler, and everything is going to be all right."

****

Lucy let out a long sigh. "Ben, would you please stop pacing. You're making me crazy."

"Sorry, I'm just nervous. Nervous, excited and...hopeful." Ben dropped onto the waiting room chair, stretched out his legs and crossed them at the ankles. "What's taking so long? It's been hours."

"I know."

Ben heard the worry in her voice, and it made him even more anxious. "I want her back, but I'm afraid. When I left...it wasn't good." He wished he could take back everything he'd said, step into Professor Willymeier's time machine and do it all differently. Unfortunately, this was real life, not actors on a stage. There was no way to take back words spoken in anger, no matter how much he regretted saying them.

All he wanted was to have Meg back—happy and healthy and brimming with life. He'd be more patient, more understanding. He'd be a better husband. He'd be a better friend.

But even if she woke up, he wasn't sure he'd ever have back the Meg he'd married. He'd learned that the person he'd fallen in love with was an illusion she'd built to protect herself, a mask to hide her real self which was too vulnerable to reveal. No one could maintain that façade forever. Over the years it slowly slipped away until he barely recognized the woman living inside.

Ben and Lucy both jumped to their feet when Dr. Beckett entered the waiting room. "I'm afraid the news isn't all good," she said. "Meg is awake and her vitals are normal. She seems to be fine for the most part."

Ben frowned. "For the most part?" What did she mean by that?

The doctor looked away, then back again. The look in her eyes told Ben he wouldn't like what she had to say next. "We ran Meg through a series of tests. She's experiencing retrograde amnesia, but there's no sign of brain damage. Her X-rays and CT scans came back clean."

Ben shook his head, trying to grasp what the doctor was saying. "Meg has amnesia?"

"Yes. Her cognitive skills are normal, and her short-term memory doesn't seem to be affected. Let's hope it's only temporary, but if it isn't..."

"What do you mean? She doesn't remember anything?"

"At the moment, no."

Ben struggled to understand. "Her memory will come back, won't it?"

Dr. Beckett lifted one shoulder in an involuntary shrug. For just a moment her professionalism dropped, and she reached out for Ben's hand, her eyes soft with compassion. "We don't know. Sometimes with trauma the brain has its own way of protecting itself. Some things may be too painful to remember."

"When can we see her?" Lucy asked.

The doctor let out a deep sigh. "I'll bring you in for a brief visit. One at a time. Just remember to keep things simple and direct. I wouldn't try to push her to remember anything. Right now, her memory is a blank slate, so be careful what you write on it."

****

Meg wasn't sure what to expect. Dr. Beckett said her husband was waiting outside. *Husband*? Would she recognize him? Would she feel anything at all? More important questions crowded her mind.

Who am I? What do I do? Who can I trust?

She heard whispering outside the door and wondered if they were talking about her. Conspiring against her? That was silly. Why would anyone conspire against her? She was being paranoid, that's all. Her fists clenched. The only thing to fear was the unknown. Answers waited on the other side of that door.

Dr. Beckett entered the room. The man beside her seemed pleasant enough, but Meg didn't recognize him at all. His eyes were filled with hope. She wished she could reassure him, but he was a stranger to her, and she had her own issues to deal with.

"This is Ben," Dr. Beckett said. "He's been here by your bedside every day."

Meg nodded, then frowned. "Every day? How long have I been unconscious?"

The doctor chose her words carefully. "You've been in a medically-induced coma to facilitate the healing process."

"How long?"

"There was extensive damage. You needed time…"

"How long?" Meg repeated, more forcefully this time.

"Twenty-one days."

Meg gasped. "Twenty-one...*three weeks*?"

Ben rushed forward and reached for her, but Meg pulled away, avoiding his touch. "I'm sorry," she said seeing the shocked expression on his face. "It's just...I don't know you. I don't even know *me* right now."

"It's all right," Dr. Beckett said. "Your memories should come back in time."

"When?"

Dr. Beckett looked from Meg to Ben and back again. "We can't be sure, but I have every expectation this condition is temporary."

Meg chewed on her lower lip and glanced at Ben, who seemed as confused as she felt.

"So," she said. "You're the husband, huh?" She couldn't say *my husband*. The words felt foreign in her mouth.

Ben nodded and reached into his pocket. He pulled a laminated picture from his wallet and held it out so she could see. "This is our wedding picture."

She stared at the photograph. The bride smiled at the camera, clasping a bouquet of pink roses. The groom stared lovingly at her as if nothing else existed in the world.

"Oh, I look so happy," she said.

"We were."

"Were?"

"Are. We *are* happy." He looked away, then back again, a strained smile on his face.

She tipped her head and stared at him. He was cute, in a boy-next-door kind of way. Kind of shy. Definitely not what she expected. His nose was Puritan straight, his hair a nondescript shade of brown that kept falling over his forehead no matter how many times he finger-combed it back. He didn't seem like her type at all, which was a strange thought. She didn't even remember what her type was, yet she instinctively knew that Ben wasn't it.

His eyes glistened with unshed tears. Her heart melted with sympathy, but nothing more. No trace of lost love, no memories of a wedding day, and no desire to recreate their honeymoon.

She lay back and closed her eyes, releasing a deep sigh.

"Maybe we should let Meg get some rest," Dr. Beckett said. She shot Ben a meaningful glance. "We have more tests to run today, so there's no sense in you hanging around."

"Okay." Ben slid the wedding picture under Meg's pillow. "I'll be back tomorrow," he murmured.

Meg remained silent. She heard one set of footsteps leave the room, then she opened her eyes. Dr. Beckett was still by her bed. "Do you need some time, or would you like to see Lucy now? She's been here every day as well."

"You said she was my best friend?"

"Yes."

"And she's been here every day? Doesn't she have a job? Oh my God, do *I* have a job? I've been here for three weeks. Was I fired?"

Meg knew she was rambling but couldn't stop herself. "I wonder what I do for a living?"

Dr. Beckett simply smiled. "Maybe that's something Lucy can tell you. Why don't I bring her in?"

"Okay."

Meg wasn't sure what to expect, but when Lucy entered the room, she looked exactly like a best friend should—open and friendly, with strawberry-blonde curls that framed a smiling face and a *Hello Kitty* tote bag. Meg liked her instantly.

Lucy walked in under Dr. Beckett's watchful eye, but as soon as she spotted Meg, she rushed forward, leaned over the side rail and gathered her up in a warm embrace. Meg stiffened at first, then settled into the embrace. It felt nice. Natural.

"I'm so glad you're awake. I've missed you so much."

"I don't..."

"I know. It's okay. We'll fill in the blanks. For now, just know I'm here for you. Whatever you need."

"Tell me," Meg implored. "Tell me what I need to know in order to get through the next few days."

Lucy pulled a chair alongside the bed. "Your name is Meg, but you know that already. You've been married to Ben for four years. I was your maid of honor."

"Four years? Do we have kids?"

Lucy stuttered, then shook her head. "Nope, no kids. Just a beast of a cat that lurks on top of your dresser and attacks people when they walk by. You're the only one who thinks it's cute. His name is Barney, and you swear you've trained him to say 'I love you,' but it just sounds like caterwauling to me."

Meg couldn't help smiling. Unlike her feelings for Ben, she felt an immediate connection with Lucy.

"So, what do I do for a living? I'd opt for princess,

but I don't see a crown, so I guess that's out of the question."

"Close," Lucy said. "You run a cupcake truck. Well, *we* do. We're business partners."

Meg was convinced Lucy was pulling her leg. "Seriously?"

"Yep. It's called Sweet Sensations. You're the creative one, and I do the books and accounting. I haven't had the heart to run it without you, but we're starting to drift into the red, and if we don't start delivering cupcakes soon, we'll lose most of our regular customers."

Meg smiled. "Cupcakes. And we're business partners. I like it."

"You should," Lucy said with a chuckle. "It was your dream. I just do the paperwork. You do all the baking and come up with new cupcake flavors, like Mustachio, Bailey's Irish Dream, Lady Amaretto, and our most popular cupcake, Tropical Sunset."

"Sounds delicious." She could see herself baking mountains of cupcakes, wearing a cute little apron while Lucy sat in front of her computer screen frowning over spreadsheets and tax forms. When she spoke, she was surprised by the wistful tone of her voice. "I wonder if I'll remember how to bake?"

"Of course, you will. You're a natural. And I'll help. That's what friends are for."

Tears welled up in Meg's eyes. "The doctor said you've been here every day."

Lucy nodded. "Like I said, that's what friends are for."

Meg tried to pull up a memory. Anything. The harder she tried, the more frustrated she became. Her brain hurt from trying to remember and every question she asked Lucy left a little footprint of pain behind.

Meg felt as if she was trying to put puzzle pieces together without a picture to go by. Here was a piece of sky, a bit of grass, something that could be a window or door. Maybe with time, the picture would be complete, but for now she grasped at every little piece of information Lucy offered.

****

Ben waited for Lucy to come out of Meg's room. It seemed as if she was in there forever. He wasn't sure if that was a good sign or not.

When Lucy finally rejoined him in the waiting room, they looked at each other like two survivors of a natural disaster. Lucy shook her head. "She doesn't remember a thing." All the pent-up emotion she'd been holding in broke through, and she collapsed in Ben's arms.

"It'll be okay," he assured her, although he wasn't completely convinced himself.

"What if she never gets her memory back?"

Ben didn't even want to consider that option. "If that happens, we'll help her remember all the good times. We'll fill in her memory for her."

Lucy sniffled, reached in her bag for a tissue, then blew her nose. "I guess. Maybe we could leave out some of the bad stuff."

"Yeah. That's a plan."

Just then Dr. Beckett entered the waiting room. "Meg is resting now," she informed them. "She has a lot to think about, and it would be best if we left her alone for tonight."

Ben started to argue, but Lucy gripped his arm and

stopped him. "The doctor is right," she said. "Anything we say now will only confuse and upset Meg. We'll come back tomorrow when she's had a chance to digest everything."

Ben shrugged. "I guess. I just feel so helpless. Normally, I'd spend the evening here with Meg and then go home and go to bed. I don't know what to do with myself."

"Well, we could go get something to eat and talk about what's going to happen once Meg is released from the hospital," Lucy replied.

Ben hadn't even thought of that. He just assumed Meg would come back home. But everything had changed. He was a stranger in her eyes. Would she feel comfortable coming back to a home and husband she didn't remember? Lucy was right. It was something they needed to talk about.

They were an unlikely pair, Ben thought as they left the hospital and walked to a nearby diner. If it wasn't for Meg, they'd have nothing at all in common. But they both wanted what was best for Meg and because of that, they needed to work together.

The diner smelled like old wood and grilled onions. Despite the appearance, the coffee was strong, and the burgers were juicy on the inside and charcoaled on the outside. It was the kind of place where they could sit and chat for as long as they wanted without anyone making them feel uncomfortable.

The waitress showed them to a table and placed two menus in front of them. Ben didn't even glance at it. "I'll have coffee and a cheeseburger."

"I'll have the same," Lucy said.

When the waitress walked away, Ben turned his

attention to Lucy. "I was thinking about what you said." He shook his head. "It'll be hard for Meg coming back home to a place she doesn't even remember."

"And a husband she doesn't remember," Lucy pointed out. "You're a stranger to her. No matter how hard you try, she won't feel comfortable being alone with a man she doesn't know."

"But…"

"I know you're her husband. And she knows that as well. But knowing it and being comfortable with it are two different things."

Ben thought about what Lucy was implying. Meg was his wife. She belonged with him in their home. But what if Lucy was right? Would his presence do more harm than good?

They paused as the waitress set two thick ceramic mugs of steaming coffee on the table. Ben wrapped his hands around the cup, letting the heat soothe and calm him, then lifted it up and inhaled the aroma. He blew a wisp of steam across the surface, then took a careful sip. The caffeine was just what he needed. "I can stay with a friend or get a hotel room," he said. "But I don't want Meg to be alone. Maybe you could stay with her until…"

"I could," Lucy said. "But it might be easier if she stayed with me. Less pressure on her to remember if she's not surrounded by pictures and reminders of your life together."

He tried not to take offense at her cavalier dismissal of the life he and Meg had built together. "You don't think that would help? Maybe one of those reminders, as you call them, could trigger her memory to return."

"Or maybe the strain of failing to remember could break her completely."

Ben didn't want to fight with Lucy. They had a common goal—they both wanted what was best for Meg. "Maybe we should just ask her where she'd be more comfortable."

Lucy agreed. When their burgers came, they ate in silence, both lost in their own thoughts.

Finally Ben spoke up and asked the question that had been haunting him since they discussed it in the hospital. "You don't think she did it on purpose?"

Lucy leaned back and gazed into the distance. "I'm Meg's best friend. Sometimes I think that's my full-time job. And don't think it's an easy job either. I did my best to protect her growing up, but there's only so much a kid can do."

Ben wondered if Lucy was avoiding the question, but he didn't stop her. Lucy knew more about Meg's past than he did and right now that was more important than trying to get Lucy to focus. "The two of you were close, right?"

Lucy nodded. "We had to be. We only had each other."

Ben watched a flurry of emotions pass over Lucy's face. She waved a hand to catch the server's attention, then pointed to her half-empty coffee cup. Ben suspected it was simply an excuse to regain control. She was hiding something, but Ben didn't know what.

Once her cup was filled and the server moved out of earshot, Lucy cleared her throat. "There was some kind of scandal or something involving Meg and her sister."

Lucy must have read the surprise on his face. "She

didn't tell you she had a sister, did she?"

He shook his head. How many other secrets had she kept from him? "June was Meg's younger sister. Quite a bit younger. The last time Meg went home she was ten. Something happened involving her sister, and they sent Meg back for good. As far as I know, that was the last contact she had with anyone in her family."

Ben suspected Lucy knew more than she let on. He wasn't sure whether to respect her for protecting Meg's secrets or shake her and demand she spill everything. How could he help his wife if he didn't know everything that led up to this tragedy?

"Meg really changed after that. It was as if a dark shroud fell over her, hiding the Meg I used to know. She became wild, rebellious. Maybe a little self-destructive."

Ben found it hard to merge this image with the woman he'd fallen in love with.

"As teenagers, I tried to protect her from herself, but she was on a one-way road going nowhere and wasn't even doing that right. She'd learned how to be tough but forgot how to be sweet. She'd learned to be aggressive but not how to compromise."

Ben nodded. He'd seen both sides of Meg's personality.

"I told you before, Meg was always attracted to the wrong kind of boys—the ones with hard, dangerous edges. Boys who charmed you and hurt you. Which is why I was surprised when she married you...Mr. Perfect."

Ben snorted. "You never did like me."'

"I never said I didn't like you," Lucy said. A good-natured smile took the edge off her words. "You're just not Meg's type. You're too…nice. Like I said, Meg was a glutton for punishment. And that included dating the wrong men. So, when you came along, I was a little surprised. It wasn't like Meg to bring home one of the good guys."

Ben tried to digest this image of the woman he'd married. He hadn't seen that rebellious side of her.

"So, to answer your question, do I think she tried to commit suicide?" Lucy asked. "Maybe. I honestly don't think so, but it's a possibility."

That wasn't what Ben wanted to hear, but he wasn't surprised. "Thank you," he said, "for being honest." He pushed the plate with his half-eaten burger aside. He'd lost his appetite. "So where do we go from here?"

"I guess we take it one day at a time," Lucy replied. "Maybe she'll have her memory back tomorrow."

"Or maybe not."

"One day at a time," Lucy reiterated. "No sense changing our routine until then. I'll go to the hospital in the morning, and you should go to work."

Ben started to argue, but Lucy stopped him. "There's no telling how much time you'll have to take off once Meg is released," she said. "Go on to work as usual, and I'll call you if there's any change."

She was right. He knew she was right. But it didn't feel right. He couldn't help but think if he were there, Meg would remember something. Anything.

****

Back home that night, Ben rolled over in bed and buried his face in Meg's pillow. It still held a hint of her gardenia shampoo. He closed his eyes and pictured her sitting on the edge of the bed, her long hair gliding across her bare back as she smoothed lotion on her legs in long, fluid strokes. He could watch her forever. Women had no idea how mysterious and seductive their nightly routine could be for a man.

He missed his wife.

It was only as he was drifting off to sleep that Ben realized he'd forgotten to ask Lucy about the man he'd seen coming out of Meg's hospital room the other night. Someone was hiding something. Did Meg have a brother he knew nothing about as well as a sister?

****

Sleep didn't come easy for Meg. Not surprising since she'd been asleep for the last three weeks. Her mind swirled with questions. Dr. Beckett had said she was in an accident but didn't elaborate. Car accident? Skiing accident? White-water rafting accident?

Did it matter? Whatever it was had stolen her memories, her entire past and every person she'd ever known. Even Ben and Lucy. They were the two people who had been by her side through the entire ordeal, according to Dr. Beckett. Her husband and best friend. Yet she'd had different reactions to each of them. She felt an immediate bond with Lucy, but the truth was, they were both strangers.

She pulled out the notebook Dr. Beckett had brought her. She opened it to the first page and smiled. There was something pristine and pure about a new notebook—a fresh start, a new beginning. She felt an immediate urge to journal. The blank page wouldn't be disappointed in her, wouldn't judge. She could make a note of information she'd learned and questions she needed to ask.

She began writing…

My name is Meg. At least that's what they tell me. Can't prove it by me. My name could be Bratwurst for all I know. I'll stick with Meg, though.

To be honest, I'm frightened. I'm trying to stay calm, but it's not easy. I've lost my memory and have to depend on other people to fill in the gaps. The problem is, these people are all strangers to me—my doctor, the nurse with the kind eyes, my best friend, and my husband. I have no memory of them.

I've smiled, nodded, and listened to their words, all the while hiding the fact that I'm scared to death. I don't know them at all.

They have a history with me, however, and it gives them an unfair advantage. For some reason, I feel it's necessary to keep my guard up. I don't know how to be me.

I'm overwhelmed with information that means nothing to me—names, dates, and events that I'm supposed to remember but don't. All I want is to find myself. Who am I?

Sometimes it feels like I'm only hearing part of the truth. But I'll smile, nod, and listen carefully, building my reality day by day, piece by piece.

After a while, her eyes grew tired. She put the notebook aside and fell into a restless slumber. At one point during the night, she opened her eyes in the darkened room and saw a shadowy figure sitting beside her bed. The woman leaned forward and smiled. Kind eyes and a familiar face.

"Gemma?"

"Yes. How are you feeling, Meg?"

"Confused. I don't remember anything."

"You remember me."

"Yes. I dreamed you. But you're real."

Gemma nodded. "I'm as real as you are."

Meg took some small comfort from her words, but fear had taken root and wasn't about to release its firm grip. "I'm afraid. What if I never get my memory back?"

"You will," Gemma assured her. She rested a cool palm on Meg's forehead and the headache that had settled there began to lift. "When you're ready it'll all come back. Don't rush it. Give your body and mind time to heal."

Time to heal. But how long? Her eyelids fluttered, and suddenly sleep felt within her grasp. "Will you stay with me?"

"Always," Gemma replied. "Everything's going to be all right."

"Promise?"

Meg felt rather than heard Gemma's reply as she finally released her worries and slipped into a dreamless sleep.

Chapter Eleven

Twenty-One Years Ago - Tinder Falls, Connecticut

Meg heard the snickers at the back of the school bus when it stopped in front of her yard. Shame colored her cheeks and whispers followed her as she stepped off the bus and made her way through the weed-crusted front yard. A rusty swing swayed in the breeze and echoed the mocking laughter of her classmates.

As always, Meg stopped at the doorway and listened before going inside. And as usual, she could hear her parents fighting. Instead of going inside, she made her way around back and into an unlocked shed that held rusted tools and shovels. She went to her secret hiding place and pulled out her favorite book about a princess and a prince and everyone living happily ever after. She really wanted to believe in happily ever after.

She stayed in the shed unnoticed until she couldn't hear shouting anymore. The only sound was the rumbling of her stomach. She hadn't eaten since breakfast, and all she'd had then was some saltine crackers and strawberry jam she'd been able to scratch together before going to school. Her parents had still been in bed sleeping off twin hangovers.

The strawberry jam was probably still on the counter where she'd left it. That's all she could think about. But she couldn't go in there. Not yet. She knew how quickly her parents' anger could be turned on her.

So she stayed in the shed until it grew dark and quiet. The thought of those crackers and jam finally propelled her out. By now, her stomach was growling, and she thought maybe it was safe to go in.

She was wrong.

Meg tip-toed inside. No sooner had she reached for the jar of jam when her mother crept up beside her. "Where've you been, Missy?" Her voice was gravel-rough.

The smell of alcohol and cigarettes, along with the pain in her shoulder made Meg wince. "Outside. Just outside."

"Don't talk to me in that tone of voice," her mother growled. She snatched the jar of jam from Meg's hands and threw it. The jar hit the wall behind Meg, showering her with shards of glass. Blood-red jam covered her hair and clothes.

She tried to run, but her mother grabbed her and wrenched her arm, nearly pulling it out of the socket. The pain was incredible, but worse than the pain was not knowing what she'd done to make her mother so angry.

Not knowing was the worst part. If you didn't know what you did wrong, then how could you avoid doing it in the first place?

Chapter Twelve

Present Day

The next day Meg was ready. She'd prepared a list of questions. Like where was the rest of her family? Why were Ben and Lucy the only visitors she'd had in the last three weeks? Didn't she have any other friends or family?

Panic fluttered in her stomach. Something didn't feel right. Maybe if she asked enough questions, she could figure it out.

Someone came in with a tray of food—coffee, oatmeal, and toast. Meg was surprised that she had an appetite and dug into the oatmeal. The coffee was weak, but serviceable. She reached for a packet of jam to put on her toast and pulled back the cover. At the sight of the strawberry jam, her stomach clenched, and a feeling of panic held her captive. The smell sent a visceral shock through her body. She tensed up, ready to flee. To where? And why?

A thought flickered through her brain, then floated away, but the emotion remained. There was no reason something as innocent as strawberry jam should send her into a panic attack, but it had.

She pushed the tray aside, no longer hungry. Even the coffee failed to entice her. She stared out the window, wondering how many times she'd be ambushed by feelings she couldn't explain, like hidden land mines in a snow-covered field.

She reached for her notebook, but there were no thoughts to record. Her mind was empty, a blank slate. Despite the rumbling of her stomach, she refused to look at the tray of food. Only when someone came and took it away, was she finally able to breathe again.

But still the words eluded her. As if with a mind of its own, she began sketching with sure, quick strokes of her pen. The image, which at first looked simply like scratches on the page, took shape in the form of a dragonfly that seemed real enough to take wing and fly off the page. She had no idea why, but the sketch gave her a feeling of peace.

Moments later, Lucy came rushing in, brightening the room with her effervescent smile. "I brought your favorite breakfast," she said. "Crullers and salted caramel macchiato."

"Salted what?"

Lucy smiled and handed her a paper cup with a corrugated cardboard band around the middle. "Coffee."

The cup felt warm and familiar in her hand. "This is my favorite, huh?"

"Yep."

Meg removed the plastic lid and raised the cup to her nose. It smelled delicious. A wisp of memory drifted up with the aroma. Before she could capture the elusive thought, it was gone. But just the fact that a memory tried to break through was a good sign, wasn't it?

The coffee had cooled enough to take a slow, deep sip. "Oh yes," she said with a sigh of contentment. "I can see why this is my favorite."

She took one of the crullers from Lucy and bit down into the light, doughy sweetness. "Oh, I like this game," she said. "What are some of my other favorite things?"

Lucy wiped a crumb from her chin. "Let's see. You collect porcelain carousel horses. Not just the little ones, either. You once rescued a full-size painted pony from an old carousel. You restored it and then donated it to Saint..." Lucy cleared her throat. "...to a local orphanage."

"That's either adorable or very weird." Meg pursed her lips. "I'm leaning toward adorable."

"Good choice." Lucy wolfed down the last bite of her cruller. "Oh, and you love '90's boy bands. I've tried my best to wean you off them, but you're a hopeless boy-band addict."

"I suppose it could be worse."

"I'm not sure how. If I have to listen to one more playlist with N Sync or The Backstreet Boys, I may commit..." Lucy stopped herself mid-sentence, a furious blush rising to her cheeks.

Meg noticed but didn't say anything. She caught something wary in Lucy's eyes. What was she hiding? Meg was determined to uncover the truth of who she was. "What do I do besides make the best cupcakes in the world?"

"Who said they were the best cupcakes in the world?"

"You did."

"Only because it's painted along the side of the truck. And on your business cards. And embroidered on your little pink apron."

"You better be lying," Meg said, trying to force down a bubble of laughter.

Lucy cracked. "Only about the apron." The two of them began laughing until tears streamed down their cheeks. And just when it seemed they'd gotten it under control, they'd look at each other and burst into hysterics again.

Lucy wrapped her arms around Meg. "God, I've missed you," she said.

Meg heard a deeper meaning lurking below the surface. It didn't seem as if Lucy was talking about just the past few weeks. There seemed more to it than that.

Shrugging off her suspicions, Meg reached inside the bag for another cruller. Halfway to her mouth, she frowned. "Crap, I'm not on a diet, am I?"

"Well, normally you start one every Monday morning. By Monday afternoon you're nose deep into a bag of M&M's. Since today is Tuesday, you're good."

"Thank God." Meg bit into the second cruller. Finding out about her likes was enjoyable so far. "Sounds like I have quite the sweet tooth. I guess that would explain the whole cupcake truck thing."

"You do love your job."

"How close am I to eating all our profits?"

Lucy laughed. "Nowhere near. Other than testing a new recipe, you pretty much steer clear of our inventory."

"Hmmm…what about leftovers?"

"Leftovers are delivered on a rotating basis to the local emergency squad, fire department and sheriff's office."

Meg wiped crumbs from the front of her hospital gown. "We're civic minded. I like that."

"There's no *we* about it. It was all your idea. I'm the accountant, remember? I wanted to sell day-old cupcakes for half price. You're the one who insisted our cupcakes would always be fresh, but none would ever go to waste."

Meg nodded. "Okay. I'm starting to like me."

The words were a jolt to Lucy's heart. How long had it been since Meg had actually liked herself? She almost hoped Meg's memories never returned. She was so much happier this way.

****

Ben had a hard time concentrating in the classroom. He'd checked his phone between classes and found a text from Lucy.

Meg is doing great today. She's upbeat, cheerful, and asking tons of questions. What should I do?

Stall her, he'd texted back. Dr. Beckett had advised them to go easy, not to dump too much information on her, but he could understand her need to know it all.

There'd been a few more texts since then--mostly Lucy touching base when Meg was called in for more tests. When his last morning class ended, Ben took his lunch outside to one of the picnic tables on the campus grounds. The teacher's lounge felt smothering with all the sympathetic looks and prying questions. With only half an hour for lunch, there wasn't time to get to the hospital and back again. He hoped some fresh air and sunshine would cheer him up.

He barely tasted his sandwich. Worries crowded his mind. What if Meg's memories didn't return? What if she never remembered the good times, their wedding and honeymoon, lazy Sunday mornings in bed with nothing but coffee and the newspaper, and warm summer nights filled with slow, sweet lovemaking? What if, after all was said and done, he couldn't make his wife fall in love with him again?

The first time was fresh and exciting and new. This time he knew where the cracks were. He knew how easily they could drift apart. He wondered if he had the energy to work that hard at a relationship again.

His thoughts were interrupted by a familiar voice. "Mind if I join you?" Sierra asked.

"No, not at all."

Sierra opened her lunch kit and took out a plastic container of salad. "I heard your wife regained consciousness. How's she doing?"

"That's the million-dollar question," Ben replied. He gathered up his half-eaten sandwich and put it back inside the bag, his appetite forgotten.

Sierra stabbed at her salad as if it had committed some heinous crime and deserved to be punished. "Well, I only have ten bucks, so give me the abbreviated version."

"Meg is awake, but she has no memory."

"She doesn't remember the accident?"

Ben took a slow, deep breath. "She doesn't remember anything. Not me, the accident or her entire life history."

"Oh my God. That's terrible."

"Maybe," Ben said with a shrug. "Maybe not. Most of her history isn't so great." Worse than he could have imagined. If only half of what Lucy had told him was true, Meg's story was one of abuse, abandonment, and betrayal. She believed she was unworthy of love. She believed everyone she loved would eventually leave her, and that she was unfit to be loved in return.

"She's estranged from her family," he admitted. They're part of the reason she's so depressed. I can't give her back that story."

"Then change it. You're the writer. Rewrite her life and give her all new memories."

She made it sound so simple. Ben remembered what the doctor had said. Meg had no memories of what came before. A clean slate. *I could, couldn't I? I could give her a life she can be proud of. I could give her the desire to live.*

His phone buzzed and Lucy's face showed up on the screen. His heart raced. "What happened? Is Meg okay?"

"Oh Ben," she said. He heard the panic in her voice. "I did something stupid. She was asking me all these questions and I slipped and mentioned her sister, now she's asking about her family. What should I do? Should I tell her the truth?"

"No." Ben remembered Dr. Beckett's warning. "Tell her that her family is out of reach. Just make something up. I don't want her getting upset."

Sierra waved to get his attention.

"Hold on a second, Lucy." He turned to Sierra.

"You said I looked like I could be her sister, remember?"

"Right, but…" Ben realized immediately what she was getting at. "No, that would be…"

"Temporary," Sierra said. "We could say I flew in as soon as I heard, but I have to get back. Just long enough to ease her suspicions and answer the question of why she doesn't have family visiting."

Ben mulled the idea over. It might work. Maybe it wasn't such a bad idea. "I don't know." He shook his head. "Let me think about it."

"Okay," Sierra pulled out a notebook and wrote down her phone number. "If you change your mind, I'm available."

Ben tried not to read more into the comment. He truly believed Sierra's motives were genuine. Still, she was a student, and he couldn't risk even a hint of impropriety.

Sierra stood and started walking away. "Wait," he said reaching for her arm. "Maybe we *could* pull this off."

"Of course, I can pull it off. I'm an actress, remember?"

"Yeah," he said, remembering her role in the play he'd seen a few nights ago. "And a good one as well."

She glowed with pride. "Plus, I took some improv classes, so if she asks me something I don't know, I can create something believable on the spot."

"Well, let's hope it doesn't go that far. I'll fill you in on the basics. Let me just..." He brought the phone back to his ear. "Lucy? Okay, here's the thing. Tell Meg her sister was out of town, but flew in as soon as she heard. She'll land later this evening and come right to the hospital."

"Huh?"

"Don't worry. I have a plan."

He ended the call and turned to Sierra. "So, let me fill you in on what you need to know about Meg's past. Here's her story."

Chapter Thirteen

Lucy met Ben in the waiting room, outside of Meg's earshot. "So, what's this about a sister?"

"It's easy," Ben said. "One of my students could easily pass for Meg's sister. I told you about her when I went to the play, didn't I?"

Lucy shrugged, a frown on her face. "Maybe you did. I don't remember."

"I did. So, Sierra is going to come in, answer all of Meg's questions about her family, and then leave in maybe a week or so." He made a wiping gesture with his hands. "Problem solved. Meg's questions are answered, and we don't have to explain why Meg doesn't have contact with her real family."

Lucy didn't look convinced.

Ben snapped his fingers. "Oh, speaking of family, I forgot to tell you I saw a strange man coming out of Meg's room the other night. He told the night nurse he was Meg's brother."

"Meg doesn't have a brother."

"I didn't think so."

"What did he look like?" Lucy asked.

Ben had to think about it to recreate the man in his memory. "Hard. Chiseled. He reminded me of that Wolverine guy."

"Hugh Jackman?"

"Yep, that's the one."

Lucy went white. "Clay," she murmured.

"Someone you know?"

Lucy nodded. "Someone we used to know."

Before she could explain, Sierra came rushing down the corridor. Lucy's eyes widened. "You weren't kidding," she said to Ben. "She looks just like Meg."

Lucy held out her hand to introduce herself. "How much do you know about Meg?"

"Just the basics," Sierra said. "Ben filled me in on pertinent facts, and dates of course. We'll have to pretend we've known each other since you're her best friend and all."

Lucy nodded. "Okay, let's get this show started."

****

Meg heard footsteps in the hall. Ben entered first, then Lucy. A third person pushed them aside and rushed forward, engulfing her in a tight embrace. "Geez, Sis," she said. "Scare the hell out of us, why dontcha?"

Meg leaned back, eyes widening.

"Wow, you really don't remember?"

Meg shook her head from side to side. "No."

"Well, in that case, Mom always liked me best."

Meg raised an eyebrow and shot right back without missing a beat. "Doubt it." She heard Lucy snicker, then glance at Ben. He nodded as something unspoken swept between them.

"I'm Sierra," she said, moving closer. "I'm your sister."

Meg shot Sierra a withering glance. "So, if you were so concerned, what took you so long to get here?"

"Of course, you don't remember. I was on a mission trip to Istanbul. Ben tried to get word to me, but communication is, well, you can imagine."

Meg's eyes narrowed. "Okay, so where are our parents then?"

"Mom had hip surgery the same day you had your accident. We didn't tell her right away because there was nothing she could do. She's still not up to traveling but promises to be here as soon as she can. You know they'd be here if they could."

Meg started to relax. It all made sense. She hadn't been abandoned by her family. Even if she didn't remember them, she still needed to know they cared. She turned her attention back to Sierra. "So, I want to know all about you."

"Well, I'm 22, much younger than you."

"I'm only 27!"

"Oh, so they told you, huh? Either way, you're the older..."

"And wiser..."

"Who's the one with the memory, me or you?"

Meg laughed. The back and forth banter felt natural, as if they'd been doing it all their lives. "Okay, tell me more."

"We grew up in a little town called Fancy Gap, a town so small there was barely room to change your mind."

"What's your worst memory?"

"Eating Spam. Not the email kind, but the pink meat in a can. You opened it with a little windy key that could tear an artery if you weren't careful." She paused and frowned. "Wait a minute. I take that back. There was the year we watched Mary Poppins and decided to jump off the upstairs deck holding umbrellas. Do you remember that?"

"Nope."

"Well, it was your idea, whether you remember or not. I was younger and idolized you, so I did whatever you did. Luckily, we survived, although you broke your arm and had to wear a cast for about a hundred years. I don't hold it against you, however."

"Well, that's good. I'd say I'm sorry, but since I don't remember any of it, that's not much good, is it? So, what's your best memory?"

"The year Dad got a bonus and took us all to Disney World. I was 8 and you were 13. You acted all cool and nonchalant when we had our picture taken with Cinderella, but you kept the framed photo on your dresser for years."

"Best friend?"

"Lucy, of course. The two of you were joined at the hip growing up. Hey, was that a trick question?"

Meg laughed. "Just looking for confirmation, that's all."

They went on like that for half an hour. Finally, Ben interrupted. "We should probably let you get some rest, Meg."

"Oh, but I'm not tired." That was a lie, but she couldn't bear for them to leave yet. There was so much more she wanted to know.

Ben was firm, however. "I'm going to see Lucy and Sierra home while you have your dinner, then I'll be back to spend the evening with you, okay?"

Meg leaned back against her pillow, suddenly realizing how tired she really was.

Sierra leaned in and kissed her cheek. "I'll be back tomorrow, okay?"

"Promise?"

Sierra reached forward and curled her finger around Meg's. "Pinky swear."

She slipped something into Meg's hand. When she was alone, Meg unfolded the piece of paper. Sierra had written her phone number on it and a note saying, "Call me anytime."

Meg smiled and held the paper to her chest. It was good to know there was someone she could count on when the world around her felt fragile and insecure.

****

Ben couldn't help feeling uncomfortable about the charade. Meg had seemed so happy, but it was all a lie.

"That was so much fun," Sierra gushed. "I like her. I really do."

"Yeah, but…" Ben grimaced. "I don't know. You're really good at this, but I'm uncomfortable with all the improvisation. I mean, if we don't keep track of our stories, we'll get caught in a lie and then what?"

"No worries," Sierra said. "We'll keep track of everything we tell her. Maybe put it in a little journal or something. What do they call that, a story bible? It'll be something we can all refer to in order to keep her story straight."

She made it sound so easy. Even Lucy seemed unfazed. "I almost hope Meg never regains her memories," she said. "She's like the old Meg that I remember. The hard edges have softened. She's funny, not melancholy; optimistic, not cynical. I just wish she could stay that way."

Ben couldn't agree more. Meg's voice was sweeter and her smile more genuine. He was reminded of the doctor saying she was a clean slate. Maybe they *could* keep her that way. Maybe they could rebuild her past so the undamaged Meg could emerge, the one he'd glimpsed when he'd fallen in love with her.

Who knew how much more she'd have become if her story had been different?

That was the thought that stayed with him all evening. Sitting with Meg that evening, he couldn't help comparing the woman before him to the wife he'd argued with a few weeks ago. She smiled when she recounted the stories Sierra had told her, there was a carefree lilt to her voice and her face glowed.

Was this the Meg that should have been if her life had been different?

The question preyed on his mind until he returned to his apartment that evening. Maybe that's what compelled him to read Meg's journal after all. Before it would have been idle curiosity. Now it was a need to protect, to know what demons chased her so he could exorcise them for good.

Reading her personal, private thoughts made Ben feel like a voyeur. Especially when he began reading about Meg's true feelings for him.

Dear Gemma,

Today is my wedding day. It should be the happiest day of my life, but something is missing.

I thought I'd found a safe place, a place where I could put all the pain behind me. I'd pushed passion aside. All passion ever led to was loss and betrayal. Better to lead a safe, uneventful life.

Uneventful? Safe? Passionless? Is that how Meg viewed their marriage? How could their interpretations be so different? And who was Gemma? He'd have to ask Lucy.

Ben is sweet, kind, and thoughtful. He's not

dangerous or impulsive, or oh-so-exciting. He's safe, a calm oasis in a churning sea where I can put all the pain behind me. That's the choice I made. Safety over passion.

Who knew being a nice guy could sound so dull? She'd settled for safety instead of excitement. He almost stopped right there, but knowing what Meg was dealing with was the first step in helping her move past it.

By the time he was done, his feelings for Meg had changed in more ways than one. What he thought he knew about her past was simply the tip of the iceberg. His heart broke for the little girl who'd been beaten by both physical and verbal abuse, who'd been shattered by a family who turned their back on her. No wonder she yearned for a safe place to heal.

He'd given her that—a marriage that was safe and calm. Or, as she called it, uneventful and passionless. He was stable and dependable; someone she could count on.

Now, more than ever, Ben was determined to keep her past a secret for as long as possible. Let her enjoy the safety and calm that she craved. Perhaps if she never recovered her memories, the nightmare would finally be over.

Guilt gripped him. He was the one thing Meg could depend on, and when she'd needed his understanding most, he'd pushed her away. Like everyone else had. Ben wished he could take it all back. If he could change things, he'd be more patient, more understanding. He'd have been there for her when she needed him most.

He sat in the silence, eyes wide in a world of shadows. Gray on gray. Meg was the one who brought color to his life. He had to find a way to make things right again.

****

Across town, Lucy had other things on her mind. She slammed her fist on Clay's door. It had taken her all night to find him, and if she got him out of bed, too damn bad.

She pounded again, muttering under her breath. "Open the damn door you son-of-a..."

Clay opened the door, took one look at Lucy and smiled. "Well, well, look who's here."

Lucy brushed past him into the apartment, ignoring his hundred-watt smile and lanky good looks.

"Come right in," Clay quipped with a sweep of his hand. "Make yourself at home."

Lucy turned and glared at him, hands on her hips. "When did you get out of jail?"

Clay sauntered to a beaten down recliner that looked as if it had come with the apartment several tenants ago. He sat, stretched out his long, denim-clad legs and crossed one scuffed cowboy boot over the other. "About a month now. I'd have sent you an invitation to my get-out-of-jail party, but I didn't have a stamp."

"Oh, cut the crap, Clay." Unlike Meg, Lucy was immune to his bad-boy charms. "What were you doing in Meg's hospital room?"

"Who said I was there?"

"Meg's husband. He described you to a T."

Clay shrugged. "So what? It's a free world, and if I want to visit an old friend in the hospital, you can't stop me. Neither can her goody-two-shoes husband. Although what she ever saw in him is beyond me."

Lucy closed the distance between them and poked her finger in the center of Clay's chest. "Stay away from Meg. Understand me? You're the last thing she needs right now."

Lucy turned and stalked to the door. Before she could leave, Clay stopped her. "How is she, Luce? Is Meg still in a coma?"

For a moment, Lucy almost believed his concern was genuine. Then she remembered what he'd put Meg through, and her heart hardened. Clay and Meg were hot and passionate for a while before Ben came into the picture, but it ended badly. She couldn't bear to see Meg hurt again.

"She's out of the coma and recovering," Lucy said, then turned and walked out the door, slamming it soundly and putting Clay back in the past where he belonged.

Chapter Fourteen

The following day, Josh pulled Ben aside in the teacher's lounge. "How are you doing?"

Ben shrugged. "Better. Meg's out of the coma and seems to be recovering. They're keeping her in the hospital for a few more days to keep an eye on the swelling. Plus, she needs some physical therapy before she can be released."

"That's great news." He draped an arm over Ben's shoulder. "But what about you? How are you doing through all of this?"

His friend's concern broke through the brave front Ben had been keeping up the last month. His shoulders lowered and his voice dropped. "I'm running on empty," he admitted. "Meg doesn't remember anything. Not the good or the bad. I'm splitting my time between the classroom and the hospital, and half the time I don't know if I'm coming or going."

Josh poured them both a cup of strong, black coffee, then gestured to a private table in the corner. "Talk to me, buddy," he said, taking a seat. "Do they think she'll get her memory back?"

Ben shook his head. He wrapped his hands around the coffee cup, drawing strength from the warmth. "They don't know. And to be honest, I'm not sure I want her to. She's different now. More like the Meg I married."

Ben smiled at the memory. Meg had been everything, but next to her, his first love was writing. He'd get up early and pound out a few pages, go to work, come home and write some more. Meg had been his number one fan even before he was published. She believed in him, and her encouragement pushed him to write better than he ever had before or since.

Those years were magical. Every now and then he'd catch a verse of an old song that shot him back into those early years. He felt the same emotions, and only then did he realize how much he'd lost.

He couldn't put his finger on the exact moment things changed. Maybe it was when they first started talking about having a family. But those years were a blur. He'd been caught up in a whirlwind of excitement—book signings, interviews, late-night meetings over drinks with his agent.

"After the book came out, Meg became quieter, more distant," he told Josh. "I didn't notice that she was slowly slipping away. I lost my wife, my inspiration, and my biggest supporter. I became a prisoner of her depression."

Ben sat back and blew out a breath. "I couldn't think, I couldn't write. Her mood swings sucked the life out of everything."

Ben raked his fingers through his hair. "Christ, I'm thirty years old. I thought by now I'd be a successful, bestselling author. Not just a one-hit wonder. I blamed Meg's depression because it was easier than blaming myself."

He shook his head. "So instead of writing, which I used to love, I teach writing to eager young students."

"And you're damn good at it."

"Don't get me wrong," Ben said, holding up a hand to ward off any arguments. "I don't hate it. As a matter of fact, I get a kick out of the way the students look up to me. My wife used to look at me that way."

"Listen," Josh said. "Why don't we go out for a few drinks tonight. After you leave the hospital. Doesn't matter how late. Just give me a call, and I'll pick you up. We'll grab some wings and a couple of beers at Cappy's."

Ben was touched. His first instinct was to decline, but when they stood, Josh clapped him on the back. "There's no sense carrying this burden all alone."

"Thanks," he said. "I appreciate it."

"Not a problem since you're buying." Josh winked then sauntered out of the teacher's lounge, leaving Ben ready to tackle his afternoon classes with a smile.

****

Meg chased Lucy out of the hospital room. "Go on, get out. There's no sense both of us being stuck in this dreary hospital room. Get out and enjoy the sunshine."

"I don't mind staying."

"Well, I do. I might want to read a book or take a nap, but I feel guilty doing that while you're watching over me like a mother hen." She smiled, taking the edge off the statement, then held up the nurse call button. "Besides, if I need something, I just click this, and someone comes running to help."

It took a while, but Meg finally convinced Lucy to leave. It felt good to finally be alone with her thoughts. Well, not counting nurses, and doctors, and patients, and visitors. But at least she didn't have someone standing over her wanting something she couldn't give them…her memory. Despite how lighthearted their visits were, Meg could sense how desperately Ben and Lucy wanted her to remember something. Anything.

She picked up the journal. Dr. Beckett had encouraged her to just write. Write anything she could remember. Anything at all. It was hopeless. She couldn't remember a thing and writing about sitting in a hospital bed seemed pointless. Why would anyone keep a journal anyway?

She turned and Ben's wedding picture slid out from under the pillow. She stared at it, trying to find a memory attached to it. Nothing. No emotion, no memories, nothing. She slipped the picture inside the pages of the journal, giving up on both counts.

Sleep eluded her. Her brain was awhirl with questions. Why weren't there other pictures of her growing up? Where was the rest of her family? When could she leave the hospital? And most important of all, would she ever get her memory back?

She lay there with her eyes closed until she heard a commotion in the hallway. She opened one eye and saw Sierra peeking into the room.

"Hi, are you awake?"

Meg sat up and pushed herself upright. "Yeah, come on in."

Sierra turned to address someone out of Meg's range of vision, then turned back to Meg. "I have a surprise for you."

She ushered in a couple who smiled at Meg with misty eyes.

The gentleman wore a Hawaiian print shirt, khaki pants and a fedora. He had a funny little Charlie Chaplin mustache. "Oh, honey, we're so sorry we couldn't get here sooner." He held the arm of a woman dressed from head to toe in petal pink, including her purse and shoes. Her hair and pearls were buttercream white. She looked like a little girl's birthday cake.

With the aid of a walker, she made her way slowly across the room. The gentleman stayed beside her, guiding her carefully. "Mother had hip surgery," he said. "We would have come sooner if we could. Ben kept us up-to-date on your progress, and as soon as Mother was cleared for travel, we got on a plane."

"Thank goodness you're all right." The woman leaned over and kissed Meg's forehead. "We've been so worried."

"I wasn't worried," the man said. "Your mother was worried. I know my girl's a survivor." He patted her hand, "Sierra told us about your memory issue. I thought, how can she not remember us? We're family."

"I'm sorry," Meg said. "I don't."

The woman had the saddest eyes Meg had ever seen in her life. "I'm Mabel," she said. "Your mother. Do you remember now?"

"No, I'm sorry."

The gentleman spoke up next. "I'm Norm." He waited, head cocked.

Sierra and Mabel looked at her expectantly, then finally said together, "Hi Norm." They looked at each other and shook their heads. Obviously, Meg was missing the punch line of a family joke.

Norm held out is hand. "I brought you something I know you're going to love."

"A diamond ring?"

He chuckled and dropped a wrapped caramel into her hand. "Your favorite."

More to please him than for any other reason, Meg

unwrapped the caramel and dropped it into her mouth. "Yum." The sweet caramel tried to tease secret memories of a doting Dad who sneaked candy to his little girl. She wanted to give this charming couple the gift of her memories, but the effort was futile.

She tried to think of something to start a conversation. The best she could come up with was asking what they did.

"I'm an inventor," Norm said.

"Oh, for crying out loud." Mabel smacked him on the arm, then turned to Meg. "He made a stick that holds the garbage can lid up."

"Well? It's an invention, isn't it?"

"Don't listen to him, Meg. He's full of baloney. Always has been, always will be."

Meg couldn't help but smile. She may not remember Mabel or Norm, but she was delighted to have them as parents. "How long have you been married?"

"Thirty-four years."

Mabel poked her husband. "Thirty-five. We just had our anniversary party. How can you not remember?"

Norm smiled and winked at Meg, as if the two of them were conspirators to a private joke. She had a feeling he purposely initiated this good-natured teasing on a regular basis. He leaned over and pecked his wife's cheek.

Mabel blushed and rolled her eyes. "Thirty-five years and he still makes me giddy," she said.

That's the kind of love I want, Meg thought. The kind that still makes you giddy after thirty-five years.

As if on cue, Ben walked in the door. "Oh, here's

Ben now," Sierra gushed. "Ben, Mom and Dad just flew in."

Ben stared from one to the other, his eyes wide and mouth open.

"I know you're surprised," Sierra interjected. "We had no idea Mom would make such a quick recovery. It's amazing, isn't it?"

Ben nodded.

Norm walked over and clapped Ben on the back. "We appreciate you keeping us in the loop, Ben. And taking such good care of our little girl." He chuckled. "You're still my favorite son-in-law."

Sierra let out an exasperated huff. "Da-ad!"

"All right, all right. I'm not trying to pressure you or anything. Just saying you're not getting any younger, that's all."

"Oh, stop it you two," Mabel chided. "Someone get me a chair so I can sit down, please. My hip is starting to throb."

Ben rushed forward and pulled a chair to the side of the bed. "Can I get you anything else?" he asked.

"A glass of water would be nice," she said, placing her purse on her lap and rooting through it. "I need to take my pills."

Ben rushed to get a glass of water. While Mabel searched for her pills, Norm made his way to the other side of the hospital bed and slipped Meg another caramel. "Shhh," he whispered. "Don't tell your mother."

Meg felt a rush of warmth rise to her chest. These people were strangers, but they loved her. She felt like the luckiest girl alive.

Ben came back with a glass of water and handed it

to Mabel, then turned to Sierra. "Could I talk to you for a minute?"

"Sure," Sierra said. "You guys get reacquainted. We'll be right back."

****

Outside Meg's room, Ben hissed, "What the hell were you thinking?"

"I was thinking Meg needed to feel grounded," Sierra said. "She keeps asking me about our family. She wants to see pictures. Oh, that reminds me, I told her all of our family pictures were lost in a fire. You might want to make a note of that."

"Good Lord. What other things are you telling her?" He jerked his head toward Meg's room. "And what about those two?"

"They're part of my acting group. You remember Norm, right? He played Professor Willymeier in the play. They're fantastic at improv, aren't they?"

Ben ran a hand over his face. "Great. More improvisation. We'll never keep our stories straight."

"Don't worry. I'm keeping notes. You can start a file and call it Meg's Story."

"But it's *not* her story. It's all made up."

"Well, she doesn't know that. And look how happy she is."

Ben couldn't argue with that. He heard her laughter all the way down the corridor. This new Meg was the person she would have been if life hadn't gotten in her way.

Sierra reached for his arm. "It's only temporary. Just to keep her from freaking out while she readjusts to life. What harm can come of it?"

Ben wasn't sure. It didn't feel right to him, but the

sound of Meg's laughter was enticing. Maybe Sierra was right.

****

Later that night, Ben laid it all out to Josh over beer and wings. "So, it's totally out of control," he said. "Sierra has invented this entire new family for Meg." He brushed his fingers through is hair. "Yeah, it's made her feel better, but what's going to happen when she figures it out?"

"I can see why you're concerned," Josh said, lifting a beer to his lips.

"We hope she gets her memory back," Ben said with a shake of his head. "But what if she doesn't?"

Josh tapped his thumb against the edge of his plate. "You know, this reminds me of a book I once read. Did you ever hear of the Neville Reader?"

"No."

Josh sat back. "According to Neville, you can rewrite your past and turn around all the bad things that happened. Think of it. We remake our memories each time we recall them. In other words, when we remember something, we're not remembering the actual event, but the last time we visited that particular memory. So, according to Neville, if we embellish the memory, that embellishment becomes part of the fabric of our past history."

"Okay, I'm not sure if I understand."

"If you alter the memory in even the slightest, the next time you remember a slightly different version. Keep altering it and soon the memory is completely different. In effect, you've changed your past and the way you react to it."

"I suppose, but…"

"Think about it," Josh said. "We do it all the time. It's called revisionist history. Have you ever told a lie so many times that you began to believe it yourself?"

"Not since high school."

Josh leaned back and barked a laugh.

"I get what you're saying," Ben said. "But this is different. Meg doesn't have any control over changing her past."

"Better still. You don't have to erase the past, just build her a new one."

Josh wasn't the first person to suggest that Ben rewrite Meg's past. Did he need any more encouragement than seeing the way Meg was now, compared to the Meg who was depressed, morose and suicidal? And what about her real family? They had no intention of being a part of her life and, as far as Ben was concerned, didn't deserve to be.

What harm would it do?

The idea lingered long after the evening ended. By the time he got home, Ben had decided to write a rough outline of Meg's fictional past, using the tools of his trade.

But first he had to hide any evidence of her past. If she accidentally ran across her journal, the entire sham would be exposed. He'd have to hide it someplace where she wouldn't find it.

Chapter Fifteen

At first Ben was non-committal. He was simply making some notes; that was all. He tried to remember some of the things Sierra had told Meg. Something about all their family pictures being lost in a fire. He scribbled some items on a bullet list. Disneyland? Disney World Yeah, Sierra had said they took a family trip. Before he knew it, Ben was in the zone, writing in a way he hadn't written in years.

Sure, it was just a bare-bones outline of Meg's pretend life, but it started to take on a life of its own. Meg was no longer his wife, but a character in a story that he had full control over.

It felt good to be writing, even if it wasn't anything that would ever be published. When he came up for air, he had five pages written. Single spaced. But there were holes in the story. He checked the time. 9:30. Still early.

He sent a text to Sierra. "I'm working on Meg's back story. Any chance you're free to flesh it out with me?"

The response came back immediately. "Sure, where do you want to meet?"

Ben thought about it for a moment. He had notes and papers spread all over his desk, with most of the outline on his computer screen. "Why don't you come over here," he said, and sent her the address. They had all day to work on the story. Meg was being released

Sunday, and he wanted everything to be perfect.

He put the kettle on to boil and searched the cupboard until he found the Earl Grey. By the time the kettle whistled, Sierra was at the door.

"That was quick," he said, letting her inside. "I'm making tea. Would you like a cup?"

"Sure."

She followed him into the kitchen and watched as he brewed the tea, then added cream and two spoonfuls of sugar to her own cup. Meg wouldn't approve, Ben thought. But then, Meg had no idea that she preferred her tea straight without cream and sugar. Should he write that in? Should he make note of all her preferences or let her find out for herself?

Sierra trailed behind Ben as he made his way to the dining room table, which was covered with notes. She placed her teacup on the table and began reading the outline on Ben's computer. "Nice," she said. "You remembered most of what I told her."

"Yeah, but there are still gaps. Those actors you got to play her parents added a lot of details I'm not aware of."

"Sorry. I just thought bringing them in would add more authenticity and stop Meg from asking so many questions. I had no idea how well they'd play the part."

"It's okay. As long as we all keep the details straight." Ben picked up a pen and paper. "So you told Meg her mother had hip surgery. Would she be up and walking around already?"

"Geez, I didn't think of that," Sierra said.

"Those are the kinds of details that could trip us up. Once I have an outline finalized, we don't veer from the script, okay? No more embellishments."

"But..."

"No buts. We keep it simple. The simpler the better."

"Okay," Sierra said. "Let me see what you have so far."

Sierra read Ben's outline, making a few corrections and additions here and there. She glanced up. "Does Meg have any other brothers and sisters?"

"Not that I know of," Ben admitted. "But no more actors. As a matter of fact, now that Meg is convinced she hasn't been abandoned by her family, I think the three of you should prepare her for the fact that you have to go back home."

"Not yet," Sierra said. "I mean, I know we planned on it being a short-term thing, but I really like Meg. I feel a connection, almost as if she's the sister I never had. And I think she needs me. She trusts me."

Sierra raised imploring eyes to Ben. "Another week, that's all. Then I'll tell her I have to get back home. Just give her a chance to acclimate to her new life first, okay?"

Ben gave in. What harm could come of it? Sierra was right. Meg needed that connection until she felt secure with him again.

"So, if I'm going to play the part of Meg's sister realistically, I should know more about her. Tell me what made you fall in love with Meg? What did you see in her? I want to know Meg the same way you do."

"I guess the first thing you should know is that there are two Megs—the light-hearted life of the party Meg and the shadow self she reveals when the mask becomes too heavy to wear."

At first, Ben had only known the Meg of light. The

other was hidden away. But she couldn't stay hidden for long. The effort required to maintain the façade was monumental and eventually the mask fell with a silent crash, revealing the deep and dark depression nothing could hide. "Eventually, the depression got the better of her. She was either high-wire high or flat-line low. There was no in between."

Sierra rested her hand over his. "I'm sorry."

Ben pulled his hand away on the pretense of reaching for his tea. He took a sip, but it had cooled off while they talked. "I believe in Meg," Ben said. "I believe in her strength. She's survived more than most people could handle, but she came through it—a little bruised, a little sad, but not beaten."

Sierra stood and carried her cup to the sink. "I only see one problem," she called over her shoulder.

"What's that?"

Sierra set her cup in the sink, then turned to face Ben. "It's all too perfect. Meg's past shouldn't be all sweetness and light. No one's life is that perfect."

"Hmmm. You may be right." Ben frowned. "Maybe I need to add more conflict."

****

Meg appreciated Lucy's thoughtfulness, but when it was time to be released from the hospital, she decided the best thing to do was go home with Ben. Perhaps her memory would be jogged surrounded by her own things.

That wasn't the case, however. They pulled up to a modest two-story house on a quiet street that could have been anywhere U.S.A. There was no flash of remembrance when they opened the door, and she found herself in a pearl-gray living room with all the

106

warmth and hominess of a glossy magazine spread. Even the coffee table magazines seemed arranged for presentation rather than reading enjoyment. The room had no personality and gave no clues to who lived here.

"Hmmm…" She ran a fingertip over the coffee table. Not a speck of dust. She felt an unreasonable urge to toss the sofa pillows out of their soldier-straight alignment. Everything was too perfect. Perfect and boring. The only sign of whimsy were the carousel horses Lucy had told her about. But even those felt staged.

A cat wandered into the room and rubbed sideways against Meg's leg. She reached down and ruffled the cat's fur. "You must be Barney," she said, remembering Lucy's description. The cat simply purred, and Meg was relieved that at least the cat didn't want anything from her other than a pet, a snuggle, and possibly a can of tuna.

She could feel Ben's eyes on her, watching for signs that she remembered anything. She hated to disappoint him but couldn't pretend. She didn't remember living here. It didn't feel as if *anyone* lived here.

The kitchen, however, was a different story. She gasped at the sight of gleaming cherry cabinets, state-of-the art appliances, and miles of counter space. "Oh, this is wonderful!"

Ben smiled. "This is the reason we bought the house. You fell in love with the kitchen at first sight."

"I'm a good cook."

"Yes, you are." A hopeful note lifted his voice. "You remember?"

"No. Lucy told me about the cupcakes. How I like

to invent new flavors." She walked around the kitchen, taking in the homey touches—a bowl of shiny red apples, the cookbook open on a wooden stand, and a well-used chopping board. Whimsical teacups in a variety of patterns and colors hung beneath the cupboard, along with a set of ornate silver measuring spoons. She smiled and peeked inside at an array of canisters filled with baking ingredients. Above the canisters, a row of well-worn cookbooks lined an open shelf, ready and waiting to be used. This room felt loved.

"What's your favorite meal?" she asked, turning to Ben.

He smiled. "Meatloaf. No one makes it like you do. You use a secret ingredient."

"What is it?"

He chuckled. "If I knew, it wouldn't be a secret, would it?"

Meg opened cabinets at random, admiring the dishes and serving plates. Although she couldn't remember doing so, something told her she'd lovingly picked out each and every piece. It felt right, even if she didn't know for sure.

"I'll make you meatloaf," she said, not so much to please him, but because she knew this was her domain. Working in the kitchen would make her feel more like herself than anything she'd done so far.

"If you're feeling up to it," Ben said. "If not, we can go out to eat. Or I can order something in." He took a deep breath and let it out with a sigh. "Would you like to see the rest of the house?"

Meg tore herself away from the kitchen and followed Ben upstairs.

"This is our room," he said.

Meg stood in the doorway. Nothing. No memories of romantic evenings or lazy Sunday mornings in that king-sized bed. She turned away, feeling like an interloper in her own life. How could she not remember the intimacies of marriage? How could she not remember the man she'd spent four years married to? And how could she possibly sleep in the same bed with a stranger?

Ben watched her face, then nodded. "I put your things in the spare bedroom," he said. "I thought you'd be more comfortable in there for now."

Meg was grateful for his understanding but tried not to show just how relieved she felt.

****

After insisting that Ben go to work the next day, Meg wandered through the house hoping something would jog her memory. She rifled through her closet. Although well-worn, none of her clothes felt familiar. The jewelry chest held items that didn't appeal to her. She wondered about the woman who needed designer clothes and flashy jewelry to feel...what? Loved? Secure? Protected?

She fingered the gold band they'd taken off her in the hospital. She slipped it onto her ring finger. It fit perfectly. She twisted it around. It didn't feel perfect. It felt foreign. She slipped it off and put it back on the dresser. She wasn't ready to wear it. Not yet.

It had been a week since she'd awakened in the hospital, and there was still no sign of her memory returning. Without the memory of courtship and marriage, the ring meant no more to her than a piece of costume jewelry.

The house was too quiet. For a moment, she regretted insisting that Ben go to work. She was a stranger in her own home. The pictures on the mantle showed a woman wearing her face, but they were moments captured in another time, another place.

Meg went to the only room that felt welcoming. She puttered around the kitchen, remembering her promise to make a meatloaf for Ben. She opened the recipe box and searched through hundreds of hand-written recipe cards filed in ways that didn't always make sense. Unfortunately, the meatloaf recipes she found contained only the most basic of ingredients.

Meg wasn't sure why it had become so important to figure out what the secret meatloaf ingredient might be. Maybe it was simply a metaphor for her entire past being a big secret, or maybe it was just the challenge of the hunt.

She searched through the collection of recipe books, uncovering slips of paper with notes scribbled on them, newspaper clippings and glossy recipes torn from magazines. It became more than a search. It became an obsession, which she clung to like a drowning man clutched a life preserver. It was as if unlocking this one secret would make everything else fall into place.

Surely her sister would know. Meg snatched up the phone and scrolled through her contacts, searching for her sister's phone number. For some reason it wasn't there. Then Meg remembered the slip of paper Sierra had given her in the hospital. It was still tucked inside her purse where she'd left it. She punched in the number and tapped her foot while the phone rang on the other end.

Finally, Sierra picked up with a brisk, "Hello?"

"Sierra, this is Meg."

Her voice changed immediately. "Sis! How are you?"

"Good. I'm home now. It's strange."

"Are your memories coming back?"

"No. Not a single one. I was hoping something would jog my memory. The rooms, a picture, something. But no."

"I'm sorry."

"Listen, the reason I'm calling is because I was hoping I shared my meatloaf recipe with you. Ben says I use some secret ingredient, but he has no idea what it is. I thought maybe you knew."

There was a pause on the other end, then Sierra laughed. "Oh, I'm sorry. You know me. I'm not much of a cook." She cleared her throat. "Let me do some digging and get back to you."

Meg slumped with disappointment. "Oh, okay. Thanks. Talk to you later."

Meg hung up and continued her quest. After a thorough search of every nook and cranny, she finally gave up. There were several recipes for meatloaf, but they were all basic. No frills, and no secret ingredients listed anywhere. She did find a receipt for the toaster oven, several expired coupons, and a grocery list marked *Lucy's birthday party*. She had no idea whether the party had come and gone, but it gave her an idea.

She scrolled through her contacts and found Lucy's number. "Hey Lucy. I have a strange request. I want to make a meatloaf to surprise Ben tonight."

"What? Isn't Ben there with you?"

"Huh? No, I told him to go to work."

"Want me to come over?"

"No. I'm fine," Meg bristled. "I don't need a babysitter."

"Oh, I just thought…"

"It's okay. Listen, the reason I called is because Ben said something about a secret ingredient I use in my meatloaf, and I can't find the recipe anywhere. You wouldn't happen to know what it is, would you?"

"Sure, I do." Lucy chuckled on the other end. "You got tipsy one night and it slipped out, but you swore me to secrecy. You said if I ever told anyone you'd shave my head while I was sleeping."

Meg was ridiculously happy to find out Lucy knew. "So, what is it?"

"I'm sworn to secrecy."

"Not from me, you knucklehead."

"I'm worried about my hair. I don't have the kind of head that's attractive shaved."

Meg couldn't help laughing along with her friend. "I promise not to shave your head. Just tell me the ingredient."

"Okay. It's nutmeg."

"Nutmeg? In meatloaf?"

"Yup. You swear by it. And to be honest, your meatloaf is second best in the world."

"Only second?"

"Yeah, there's this little Amish restaurant that has you beat, but only by a slim margin. They haven't told me their secret ingredient, however, so you get points for sharing."

They fell into the familiar banter Meg remembered from the hospital. It felt good. It felt comfortable.

"Thanks, Lucy. Listen, if you're not doing

anything tonight, why don't you come over for dinner. You and Ben can test out my meatloaf and tell me if it's as good as you remember."

Lucy's voice brightened. "I'd love that. I'll bring dessert. How's six o'clock?"

"Perfect. See you then."

After ending the call, Meg gathered her ingredients. Most meatloaf recipes are the same—ground beef, eggs and some kind of filler, either crackers, corn flakes or breadcrumbs. Meg didn't think it mattered much, so she simply used what she had on hand. She added salt, pepper, and a pinch of nutmeg to the mixture, hoping that was enough before she put the loaf aside to bake later. She peeled potatoes and prepared a salad, then set the table with the pretty china in the cabinet.

She was admiring her work and feeling a sense of accomplishment when the phone rang. It was Sierra. "I did some research," she said. "According to Mom, your secret ingredient is horseradish."

"Horseradish?" Meg frowned. "Are you sure?"

"Positive. Just don't add too much. It has a kick."

"Okay. Thanks."

"Any time," Sierra said. "Listen, I was thinking of going shopping tomorrow. Want to come with me?"

"Okay."

They made arrangements, then Meg hung up, a feeling of unease in her stomach. Horseradish or nutmeg? Someone was lying. But who? And why would they lie over something so inconsequential?

More importantly, how could she uncover a lie when she didn't even know the truth?

****

Ben hated leaving Meg home alone, but she'd insisted he go to work. Since he'd already taken too much time off when she was in the hospital, he agreed, but left her with a list of instructions to follow. He only hoped he hadn't forgotten anything that might upset her. The cradle was stored in the basement. And her journal—he opened his top drawer and checked—was safely hidden in his classroom desk. What could go wrong?

He fingered the journal holding all of Meg's secrets. Could he risk having her discover the truth about her past?

A sound caught his attention, and he glanced up to see Sierra standing in the doorway. He was taken again by how much she looked like Meg had when they'd first met. Sierra smiled. "Got a minute?"

Ben slid the journal back into the drawer. "I have a few, as a matter of fact. My next class isn't for...he glanced at the clock...another twenty minutes." He gestured for her to come into the classroom.

"Good. I wanted to talk to you about Meg." Sierra wore something light and breezy that flowed around her. She seemed to float into the room rather than walk. With incredible grace, she pulled a chair up to the desk and sat across from him. "Meg called me this morning. She wanted to know something about a secret ingredient in her meatloaf." Sierra shook her head. "I had no idea what it might be, of course. But I did some investigating online and found some people add horseradish, so I called her back and told her that was her secret ingredient."

"Horseradish?" Ben shook his head. "I don't even think Meg likes horseradish."

"Well, it's going to be your favorite now. At least when you taste the meatloaf she's making you for dinner."

Ben nodded. "Okay. Thanks for telling me."

Sierra stood and turned to leave, then stopped. "Oh," she called over her shoulder. "We're going shopping tomorrow."

"Who? You and Meg?"

"Yes, me and Meg. I'll pick her up after my last class tomorrow."

"Why?"

Sierra smiled sweetly. "Because that's what sisters do."

She breezed out the door before Ben could question her further. He clenched and unclenched his fingers. This was getting out of control. The more Sierra improvised, the harder it was to keep the facts straight. He should put a stop to it now, before it went too far.

But what about Meg? She was doing so well. Granted she'd only been home one day, but he hadn't seen any signs of depression. The despondent Meg he'd been living with the last few years had disappeared, replaced by a light, carefree Meg. Once she settled in to her new life, it could only get better.

Unless she regained her memory.

Chapter Sixteen

It felt as if the walls were closing in around her. All Meg wanted to do was escape, or at the very least get out of the house and clear her head. She checked the time. There were still a few hours to kill before it was time to put dinner in the oven. When Ben had driven her home from the hospital, she'd noticed a small park only a short distance away, and the walk would do her good.

Outside, it was a perfect June day. Not too hot yet, with a whisper of a breeze. A brilliant array of flowers dotted the apartments along the street. Meg inhaled, breathing in the fresh summer air.

Although the park was only a few short blocks away, Meg was winded when she reached it. The days spent in a hospital bed had taken a toll on her. She rested on a bench overlooking a small pond, watching as people tossed bread cubes to waiting ducks. The sound of laughter floated on the air as children on swings shouted, "Higher, Mommy, higher!"

The bench dipped as someone sat beside her. Meg turned and her heart expanded with the first honest emotion she'd felt all day as she recognized the woman beside her.

"It's Gemma, right?

The woman nodded.

Meg shook her head as a wisp of memory floated

by. "Did I dream you or remember you?"

Gemma smiled. "A little of both." She placed a gentle hand on Meg's shoulder. "But that's not important right now. I thought I'd find you here."

"You did? Why?"

"It's your favorite place to think and dream." Gemma leaned forward and pointed to a metal plaque on the bench that Meg hadn't noticed before. She read the inscription aloud. "Everything will be all right in the end. If it's not all right, it is not yet the end."

At Meg's blank stare, Gemma explained. "It's a line from your favorite movie, *The Best Exotic Marigold Hotel.*

Meg filed that information away. She had a favorite movie. Let's see who else knew that. She let out a slow sigh. "I can't remember anything, Gemma. Not my favorite movie, my secret meatloaf ingredient, not my husband, my friends, my cat...nothing. I don't remember anything about *me.* "

Gemma took her hand and held it tight. "I know, Meg. I know. But sometimes memories can blur our clarity. They keep us mired in the past rather than clear to see the future." She lifted Meg's hand and pressed it against her chest. "I want you to think with your heart, not your head," she said, looking deep into Meg's eyes. "Trust your instincts."

"But what if I never remember?"

Gemma shook her head. "The past is unimportant. It's over and done. You can let it affect the things you do today, or you can let it go. It's your choice."

Meg was mulling that over when a flash of color caught her attention. A dragonfly landed on the arm of the bench. "Oh, look, a dragonfly!"

Gemma smiled. "It's a good sign. Dragonflies are a symbol of transformation, letting go of past illusions that limit growth and change. But," she cautioned, holding out her finger for the dragonfly to land on, "they also warn us to be on the lookout for falsehoods, illusions, and deceit."

Yes, Meg thought. So, she wasn't being paranoid after all. There were people around her who would deceive her and lie to her. She couldn't trust anyone until she had her own memory back.

The dragonfly flew away, hovering over the water for a moment to dance with its own reflection, then flying away in a shimmery blur of blues and greens and violet shades.

"Beautiful, isn't it?" Meg turned her head, but Gemma was gone. She'd disappeared without a sound. Meg didn't feel alone, however. She knew that Gemma would be there whenever she was needed.

"It's okay," she whispered to the breeze. "It's not the end yet, is it?"

****

Both Ben and Lucy raved about the meatloaf that evening. That meant Sierra was the one lying to her, Meg deduced. But why?

"So, the meatloaf was all right?" she asked, clearing the empty plates from the table.

"Perfect," Lucy said.

Ben nodded and rubbed his belly. "Delicious. But…"

Both Meg and Lucy glanced at him.

He shrugged. "I think it could use just a touch more horseradish."

Lucy's mouth opened, then closed again. She

shook her head. "Tasted fine to me." She got up to help Meg clear the dishes.

"I'm not saying it wasn't good," Ben said. "Just seemed like a little something was missing, that's all."

An odd look passed between Lucy and Ben. Meg wasn't quite sure what it meant, but it wasn't the first time she'd caught them silently communicating. She had more important things on her mind, however. If Sierra was telling the truth, then Lucy was lying. Or maybe she had two secret ingredients. But now that the seed of doubt had been planted, Meg was determined to flush out the lies.

While Ben finished clearing the table, Meg and Lucy loaded the dishwasher. "I saw some photos of our wedding on the wall," Meg said. "Where did we go on our honeymoon?"

Lucy replied. "Ben whisked you off to Jamaica. I still haven't forgiven him for not letting me tag along. I would have loved to go to Jamaica." She did a little shuffle around the kitchen, singing a catchy tune, "... every little thing's gonna be all right."

Meg frowned. Hadn't Gemma just said that? She wanted to ask Lucy about Gemma, but something stopped her. Maybe she could have secrets too. At least until she knew for sure who she could trust.

Lucy stopped dancing and gave Meg an odd look. She lifted her hands palm up and tipped her head questioningly. "Bob Marley?"

Meg shook her head. "I don't know who that is."

"God, you have so much to catch up on." Lucy rambled on. "Anyway, I'd have gone to Jamaica in a heartbeat. She put on an exaggerated Jamaican accent. "Drink me some island rum, smoke a little Jamaican gold, and get my groove on with a dreadlocked Rastafarian. Ya mon."

Meg couldn't help but laugh. "You wouldn't do any of that."

"I might. You don't know me."

They both stopped at that, and the silence lasted a heartbeat too long as the meaning of what Lucy had just said sunk in.

"Anyway," Lucy continued. "I have a wild side."

"I'm sure. Wild like in bed by ten o'clock, I bet."

"Eleven," Lucy countered. "But only because I need my beauty sleep."

Meg wrapped an arm around Lucy's shoulder. "You're beautiful just the way you are."

Lucy shook her head. "You're the only one who seems to think so."

As comfortable as she felt, she had to admit that Lucy was right about one thing. She *didn't* know her. She may have once, but that memory was wiped clean. Just because she felt comfortable with Lucy didn't mean she could trust her one hundred percent.

Meg wondered if she'd always been this paranoid, or if it was a byproduct of her amnesia.

She gave Lucy a hug. "I was only teasing you," she said. "Maybe you do have a wild side." She stared off into the distance. "Maybe we both do."

Lucy's voice dropped to a conspiratorial whisper. "What do you mean?"

"I don't know." Meg shook her head. "Sometimes I feel jittery, you know? Like an animal that's trapped in a cage and yearns to run free." She glanced around the kitchen. "I have everything a woman could want. But it doesn't feel right. And Ben. He seems sweet and thoughtful, but where's the passion? I don't feel anything."

She didn't know who she was or where she came from, but she knew one thing for sure—Ben wasn't the kind of man she'd date, let alone marry. He was safe, normal, boring, while something inside her craved excitement and passion.

She glanced in the doorway and saw Ben staring at her. She looked away and went back to loading the dishwasher. When she looked back again, he was gone.

Chapter Seventeen

Eleven Years Ago - St. Ophelia's Home for Girls

Quiet as a mouse, Meg reached under her bed for the backpack that held all of her earthly possessions. She didn't dare turn on the light or make a sound. Lucy was usually asleep by ten o'clock, which is why she'd told Clay to wait until midnight to come for her.

The latch on the window opened with a dull click. Meg held her breath, but there was enough moonlight to show Lucy sit up in her bed across the room. "What are you doing, Meg?"

"Shhh. Nothing. Go back to sleep."

Lucy's voice was soft and filled with desperation. "Please don't go, Meg. Don't leave me here alone."

"I have to. Now go back to sleep, Lucy Goosy."

Lucy rubbed her eyes and frowned. "It's that boy, isn't it? Clay. He's nothing but trouble, Meg. You're not running away with him, are you?"

"He loves me."

"Oh Meg. You're only sixteen."

"I'll be seventeen in a few months. I'm almost an adult." Meg opened the window, no longer concerned about making noise.

Lucy's voice trembled. "If you do this, Meg, I'll never speak to you again."

Meg stared back defiantly, then rushed across the

room and wrapped her arms around her friend. "Yes you will, because we're blood sisters and blood sisters are forever, remember?"

Lucy shrugged.

Meg put her face close to Lucy's. "Say it with me."

They repeated the vow in tandem. "When we're apart and when we're together, we'll always remain blood sisters forever."

Meg kissed her on the cheek. "I have to go now. But I'll write and I'll call. I promise."

With that she turned and rushed across the room to the window, dropping her backpack first, then making the short hop to the ground outside. A crisp layer of frost covered the ground, and the air held the first chill of winter's approach. She raced down to the end of the drive where Clay was waiting as they'd planned. Just seeing him made her heart race. He was only six months older than she was, yet he seemed so worldly, so self-assured. And so damn sexy. She'd already decided that he was going to be her first and only lover.

She rushed into his arms, and he swooped her up, leaving a trail of ticklish kisses down her neck and shoulder. "You scared me," he said, coming up for air. "I was afraid you'd changed your mind."

How could he even think that? Every nerve, every cell of her body was pulled to him like a magnet. She couldn't imagine a life without him. He ground his hips against her and she moaned, wanting everything he had to give her. If their need to escape from the grounds of St. Ophelia's hadn't been so great, she'd have pulled him to the ground right then and there to finally prove her love and devotion.

He pulled away with an audible groan and reached

over to retrieve a helmet from the back of his motorcycle. He put it on her and tightened the strap, then smiled as her head tipped to the side from the weight of the helmet. "You'll get used to it," he said. "Gotta keep my girl safe."

My girl. The words fluttered in her heart, tightened her belly, and sent heat to her center. "I'll be your girl forever, Clay," she whispered, with the sacredness of a vow. "Forever and always."

He leaned forward and kissed the tip of her nose, then put his own helmet on and helped her climb onto the back of the motorcycle. She wrapped her arms around his waist, and they took off, leaving St. Ophelia's behind in a cloud of dust.

Twenty minutes later, they crossed the state line into Massachusetts. Clay pulled up to a roadside motel, which consisted of a row of small cabins, each with a single plastic lawn chair out front.

Clay pulled up to the office and turned off the bike. "Wait here, doll," he said. "I'll be right back."

Meg unhooked her helmet and shook her hair out. She felt wild and adventurous. Clay had that effect on her. As long as he was by her side, she knew that anything was possible.

To prove it, he sauntered out of the office, holding up a set of keys. "Cabin seven," he said. "Which just happens to be my lucky number."

He hopped onto the bike, started it up again and drove the short distance to their cabin for the night. The inside was surprisingly clean. There was a dresser and mirror, a television, night stand and one bed.

One bed!

Meg suddenly felt shy, the quiet filled with a sense

of expectancy. What happened here tonight would change her life forever. There'd be no going back.

She walked across the room and turned on the radio on the bedside table, fiddling the dial until she found a pop station. When she turned back, Clay was pulling some cards out of his wallet.

"Tomorrow's another travel day," he said. "We'll take Route 7 through Massachusetts, into Vermont, and then finally over the Canadian border. Once we're in Canada, we're free and clear."

He crossed the room and handed one of the cards to Meg. It was a fake I.D. "Your name is Ruby now," he said. "Ruby Valencia." He took her hand. "And I'm your loving husband, Rick Valencia."

Husband. A thrill rippled through her body. "Rick and Ruby?"

He shrugged. "I didn't get to choose the names. But you'll make a luscious Ruby."

Meg glanced at the I.D. card and counted the years from the birth date listed. "Twenty-one? I don't look twenty-one."

Clay pulled her close. He unbuttoned the top button of her blouse. "Baby, with that body you can easily pass for twenty-one. I promise you." He unbuttoned the second button, nibbled her neck, and whispered. "The hottest twenty-one-year-old in the world, Ruby."

The way he growled "Ruby" made her wish she'd been born with that name.

"Say it again," she moaned, melting into his embrace.

"Ruby." He freed her breast from her shirt and gave it a gentle squeeze. "Ruby." He slid his other hand down to the curve of her lower back and pulled her tight against his erection. "Ruby." He nipped the side of her neck, drawing a moan from her lips.

Any reservations she may have had dissolved in the heat of his touch. He lifted his head and smiled. "Listen, babe. They're playing our song."

It was one of Meg's favorite bands, Boyz II Men.

Oh yes.

Clay lifted her and carried her to the bed, singing softly in her ear. "I'll make love to you, like you want me to…"

Chapter Eighteen

Present Day

The next morning, Ben slipped out of bed early while Meg was still asleep. He had an hour before he had to leave for work and his mind was swirling with ideas. He made a cup of coffee and went down to the basement where he had a small desk in what he liked to call "his writing corner." He opened his laptop, anxious to begin.

When was the last time he'd felt the urge to write? He couldn't remember. His muse had abandoned him, and he hadn't felt creative in months, maybe years. Now, finally, he had a story to tell. But this was different. This was his life...or a fairytale version.

At first, he'd only intended to set the facts down into some kind of story bible he could give to Lucy and Sierra. That way they would be sure to keep their facts straight and not get tripped up on some small piece of information one of them was unaware of.

But soon the character he was writing about began to speak to him. He felt that familiar rush of inspiration, the need to discover more about the person developing on the page. Ideas came rushing to him and he wrote feverishly. He'd forgotten what it felt like to be totally in the flow.

Meg's new story took on a life of its own. He

embellished details until the character he created became more real to him than the wife he'd known all these years. Her tics and traits were endearing, her character flawless. She was every man's dream and every woman's best friend.

He continued writing, caught up in the imaginary story of the way things could have been.

"Not Chinese again," Ben said with an indulgent smile.

"I can't help it," Meg replied. "I'm addicted to teriyaki sauce."

"I'll buy you a bottle."

"Oh, come on," she said. "It'll be my treat."

Ben caved in. He really couldn't complain. He liked Chinese food as much as Meg did, and Lucky Yum Yum's buffet was one of their favorite places to eat. He'd just hoped for something with a little more class to pop the question tonight, but Meg had shot down each and every one of his dinner suggestions. So Chinese it would be.

Ben imagined himself telling the story of their engagement for years to come. "It was her choice to go for Chinese," he'd say. "I'd have preferred dinner by candlelight, but whatever Meg wants, Meg gets." Then she'd smile at him with a look of adoration.

At least that's how it went in his own imagination.

And everything went just as he'd imagined it would, right up to the moment their fortune cookies arrived. Ben snapped his open first and read, "All of your questions will soon be answered."

Well, that was encouraging. He fingered the ring in his pocket while Meg opened her cookie. "What's it say?"

She smiled as she read the fortune. "The decisions you make today will change your life forever."

"That's true," he said. He slid out of the booth and bent down on one knee. "Meg, I can't imagine living without you, even if you do have a weird addiction for Chinese food. If you'll marry me, I promise to love you forever, and we'll spend every anniversary here at the Chinese buffet."

Meg laughed and threw her arms around Ben. "Of course, I'll marry you. I can't imagine living without you. Or Chinese food."

Meg saved the fortune cookie predictions and taped them in their wedding album as a reminder of the day she'd made the best decision of her life.

Ben saved the file, sat back, and stretched. Maybe he'd taken a little creative license with the scene, but his marriage proposal had gone something like that. Granted the messages in the fortune cookies were a little more mundane, but this was his story and he'd write it however he wanted. If the truth was a little less romantic, who would know?

He glanced at the clock and realized he was almost late for work. As much as he hated leaving while the ideas were so fresh in his mind, he had to stop. There would be plenty of time to write later that evening since Sierra was taking Meg for what she called "a girls' night out".

He closed the laptop, first making sure to password protect his files. It wouldn't do for Meg to discover that her entire life story was simply something he'd created.

****

The house was quiet. Ben had already left for work, and Sierra wouldn't be picking her up until later that afternoon. Meg had the entire day to investigate.

She went through a stack of magazines beside a floral print lounge chair. Obviously, this was her favorite spot to read. She couldn't imagine Ben sitting in a frilly tufted chair. But then again, she couldn't imagine herself sitting there either. She rifled through the magazines—women's this and women's that, magazines about homes and magazines about gardens, along with good, better, and best housekeeping.

This was her life? Cupcakes and housekeeping magazines? Where was the drama? Where was the excitement?

She stacked the magazines back in an orderly pile and decided to do a load of laundry to pass the time. At least she'd feel useful. She wondered how she knew enough to separate whites and darks yet couldn't remember buying the clothes that needed to be washed. She was sure the doctor had a medical answer for that, but Meg suspected maybe all those housekeeping magazines had made more of an impression on her than her real life had.

She brought the laundry down into the basement. The washer and dryer were tucked in one corner. Across the room was a well-worn couch and TV stand. Maybe this was Ben's man cave, a place where he could kick back with his buddies and watch sports. She didn't even know if Ben liked sports. Or if he had buddies for that matter. She'd been too involved with herself to ask.

Then she saw Ben's laptop and realized this was probably where he came to write so he wouldn't disturb her. Lucy said Ben had written a book. She made a mental note to read it. Maybe she could find some clues inside.

She noticed something tucked in the corner covered with a sheet and curiosity got the better of her. She lifted one corner of the sheet, surprised to see an antique cradle underneath.

Questions flooded her mind. Whose cradle was it? Had they lost a child? Why was the cradle hidden in the basement?

She ran her fingers over the smooth wood and noticed a stain the color of old blood on one of the rails. A chill rippled down her spine and sweat broke out on her forehead. Every one of her senses told her something bad had happened. Why was there blood? Had a child been hurt? Her breath came in shallow gasps. She felt dark memories trying to break loose and rise to the surface. A voice in her head warned her away...*no, no, no.*

A dark memory tried to catch her attention. It floated in wisps and mist, raising questions without answers. Something about a child. A little girl. She was in danger, There was blood. *No, no, no*, the voice in her head shouted. *Don't think about it. Don't try to remember.*

She threw the sheet back over the cradle and rushed upstairs, as if chased by demons. Her heart pounded and an ominous shroud fell over her. *Panic attack*, she assured herself. That's all it was. A panic attack.

But why? Why would a cradle bring on such a sudden and severe panic attack? Meg's first instinct was to call the counselor Dr. Beckett had recommended. But that meant getting in a car and driving, something she hadn't done since her accident. It was something she'd have to face eventually, but she wasn't sure now was the right time.

She could call Lucy or Sierra and ask them why she had such a severe reaction to something as simple as a baby's cradle, but she was pretty sure they'd both be evasive and sugar-coat her fears. Everyone treated her as if she was made of delicate bone china. Everyone except Gemma, who was the one person Meg felt on a deep, instinctive level that she could trust. But how could she get in touch with her?

What was Gemma's last name? It started with an I. She was sure of it. But for the life of her, Meg couldn't remember. Damn it!

She scrolled through the contacts on her phone – Ingram, Irvine, Ingargiola. None of them rang a bell. She closed her eyes and tried to will the name to come to her. The harder she tried, the more distant it felt. She'd just have to wait and ask Ben later that night.

She poured a glass of lemonade and brought it out to the front porch where a porch swing moved lazily in the breeze. Somehow, she knew this was one of her favorite places to relax. She wondered how many nights she and Ben had sat here talking long into the evening. Or maybe it was just her own special place to sit and meditate. Even the squeak and squeal of the chains felt familiar. Comforting. A memory floated to the surface, but the harder she tried to grasp it, the further it faded. Before she could grasp it completely, a dragonfly drew her attention away, flying lazily on shimmery wings.

A soft breeze whispered in her ear. Although she didn't recognize the words, her lips curled up in a smile. It was comforting as a soft lullaby. The hypnotic rocking chair squeaked on the wooden floorboards as she rocked forward and back, forward and back, lulling her into a dream-like state.

Who could she talk to? She wanted someone she could trust someone she could tell her secrets to, someone who cared about what she was going through. She closed her eyes and drifted.

It could have been moments or hours later when she opened her eyes to find Gemma sitting across from her, a smile of welcome on her face. Meg blinked and sat forward, returning the smile. Seeing Gemma was like an answer to a prayer.

"You must have read my mind," she cried. "I was just thinking about you."

"Is everything all right?"

"Yes, I just needed to talk to someone." She yawned and wiped the sleep from her eyes. "Can I get you something to drink?"

Gemma smiled and shook her head. "No, I'm fine. What about you? Is something wrong?"

"Something? Everything's wrong." Meg took a seat across from Gemma. "I feel like there's something I need to remember. Something important. But it's just out of reach."

Gemma nodded. "Maybe you shouldn't try so hard. When you're ready to remember, you will."

"But I saw this cradle downstairs, and there was blood on it, and I had this sudden feeling like I'd done something terrible, but I couldn't remember." A shiver rippled through her body and tears stung her eyes. "I felt overcome with guilt and shame. I can't shake the feeling that I hurt someone. A child."

Gemma took her hands. "Meg. Do you feel like the kind of person who would harm someone else?

Especially a child?"

Meg took a deep breath. "No. Never." It was the truth. Somehow, she knew she could never have done something so terrible. "I'm not that kind of person." And she knew, deep down inside, that that was the truth.

"Trust your instincts," Gemma said.

"I just wish I had my memories to rely on."

"Memories are sometimes unreliable," Gemma said. "They fool us into thinking what we remember is the truth of who we are. Use this opportunity to find out who you really are."

"I don't understand what you mean by that."

"We're born a blank slate, Meg. How we're raised helps determine who we become, and sometimes that changes who we were meant to be." Gemma squeezed Meg's hand. "You're a blank slate once again. Instead of trying to figure out what was once on that slate, maybe you can fill it up with new experiences, new memories. Start fresh, Meg. Start right here and now."

Meg shook her head. "But there's no need. I've had a wonderful life." Something about that statement rang false, however. "Haven't I?"

"Does it matter? If all we have is the here and now, then our past can no longer define us."

It wasn't the answer Meg was hoping for, but something about Gemma's attitude was so soothing that her worries no longer seemed important. The panic had subsided, replaced by a feeling of relief. Whatever memories were hidden in the past could stay in the past. All she had was the here and now, and that was enough.

It was only after Gemma left that Meg realized she'd forgotten to ask how she could get in touch with her again. Whether memory or instinct, Meg knew that Gemma would always be there when she needed her.

Chapter Nineteen

Meg discovered something new about herself that afternoon. Turned out she loved to shop. And Sierra was the perfect shopping partner. Meg tried on wild, bohemian dresses and dangling necklaces—clothes that felt more comfortable than the "soccer mom" outfits she'd found lined up in her closet.

"That one is fantastic on you!"

Meg turned and looked at herself in the dressing room mirror. Sierra was right. The dress, with its flowing skirt and muted print, brought out the color in her cheeks and made her look tall, lean, and romantic.

"I'll add it to the pile," Sierra offered.

"No." Meg gave her reflection the once over in the mirror. "I think I'll just wear this one home."

Sierra nodded. "Good choice." She dragged her to the cashier, who clipped the price tag from the dress she was wearing and winked. "It looks great on you," she said as she rang up the rest of Meg's purchases.

Meg had a moment of concern when the bill was tallied, but Ben had told her not to worry. Still, she made a mental note to talk to him about their finances. How much did a teacher make? Probably not that much. Maybe it was time she and Lucy started up the cupcake truck again to supplement his salary. Then she wouldn't feel guilty for buying new clothes when the ones in her closet were perfectly fine. Boring, but fine.

Their next stop was a kitchen supply store where Meg spent almost as much on kitchen items as she had on clothes. "I love this shopping center," she said as they made their way to an enormous bookstore. "Shouldn't we be getting home soon?" she asked.

"Nope." Sierra led her into the bookstore. "I told Ben it was a girls' night out, and he was in charge of his own dinner tonight. We're heading to my cousin's place after this for dinner and drinks."

"We have a cousin?" Meg asked.

Sierra seemed momentarily flustered, but quickly filled Meg in. "Yeah, um…Luke. He owns the Ship's Pub downtown. Great food. Local band. And he makes a fantastic Bloody Mary."

"Do I like Bloody Marys?"

"Nope. But I do. You drink some wimpy white wine."

Meg nodded. "Sounds like me. Maybe I'll be adventurous tonight and try something new. What would you suggest?"

Sierra gave her a devilish grin. "Tequila!"

"Challenge accepted." Meg hoped she wouldn't regret it in the morning. Maybe she'd better stick to her wimpy wine, as Sierra called it.

"Listen," Sierra said. "I have to make a quick phone call. Why don't you browse around for a bit, and I'll find you when I'm done."

The books beckoned her with their glossy covers and tantalizing blurbs. "What do I like to read?" she asked.

"Oh, a little bit of everything—romance, mystery, fantasy. You like them all."

It didn't take much to convince her. Meg wandered

the aisles, pulling books out and reading back covers. Soon she had an armful of books she intended to buy to replace all of those magazines she'd found earlier. She turned a corner and caught the eye of another customer who quickly looked away. There was something predatory about him. Had she seen him before? Paranoia sent her skittering in the opposite direction, convinced the dark-haired man was following her.

At one point, Meg noticed Sierra talking on her cell phone. Meg waved and gestured to her books, then pointed to the check-out counter. Sierra nodded and mouthed she'd be right there, then went back to her conversation.

Meg paid for her purchases, then waited for Sierra to do the same. "What did you get?" she asked when Sierra joined her.

"Oh, just some self-help book. How about you?"

"Escapist fiction. I seem to have a lot of time on my hands these days."

"Lucky you," Sierra said without a hint of irony.

Meg was still uncomfortable behind the wheel because of her head injury, so she'd been grateful when Sierra had offered to drive. They'd parked a few blocks away and walked past outdoor cafes, coffee shops and boutiques on the way to Sierra's car. Even though Meg knew she'd probably walked these same streets dozens of times before her amnesia, the sights and sounds were new and delightful to her. Had she shopped there before? Eaten at that restaurant? It wasn't just the big things she'd forgotten, but the everyday little things that made up a life.

When they reached Sierra's car they loaded their purchases into the trunk and set off again. Sierra bubbled with excitement, while Meg found her energy level flagging. She hadn't realized just how much the accident and subsequent stay in the hospital had taken out of her. A low-grade headache held squatter's rights, threatening to explode into a full-grown migraine.

Meg hated to admit she would rather go home and take a nap. Sierra was so excited about going to the pub, it would be a shame to let her down.

So they went, and Meg was glad they did, at least initially. The pub was cozy and warm in a dimly-lit kind of way. Luke met them at the door, first embracing Sierra, then he turned to Meg and lifted her off the ground in a massive bear hug. "How you doing, little cuz?"

Her first instinct was to lie, to say she was fine. But that wasn't true, and she was getting tired of pretending. "I'm on shaky ground...*cuz.*"

He held her gaze for a long moment, then lowered her to her feet again. "That's to be expected," he said. "You've been through a lot." Something about the gentle way he held her, the kindness in his eyes, made her feel safe and protected. "What can I do?"

Meg smiled. "Sierra says you make the best hamburger in the world."

Luke threw one arm around Sierra's shoulder. "She speaks the truth. Pure Angus beef with cheddar, Swiss cheese, bacon, sautéed onions and mushrooms, then topped with a fried egg."

"A fried egg?"

"Trust me. You'll love it."

Somehow Meg doubted that.

"I'll throw in a side of fried pickles," he offered. "No charge."

"No thanks."

Luke pretended he was shot through the heart. "I'm deeply wounded."

Sierra linked arms with Meg and led the bar. "He'll get over it. You never liked the pickles anyway." She turned and called over her shoulder to Luke. "Two Krakens with seasoned fries."

Meg slid onto a tall stool. "So, Luke. Is he on our mother's side or...?"

"Dad's side. His brother's son." Sierra made a production out of studying the menu, which Meg found strange since they'd already ordered. Sierra glanced up, then back at the menu. "I was thinking of ordering an appetizer. They have calamari." Sierra closed the menu and smiled. "Interested?"

"No. I think I've used up my adventure quota for the day."

Luke ambled up to their table with two frosty glasses of beer. He placed them on the table and jerked his head across the room. "The band's just setting up. They're pretty good. Your order's in, so take your time and enjoy the music." He winked at Meg, then turned and walked away.

Meg lifted the glass to her lips. She took a long, deep swallow, letting the cold brew bubble down her throat, then wiped her lips with the back of her hand. "Oh, that's good."

Sierra did the same, then set her glass on the table. "I'll be right back," she said. "Ladies' room."

Sierra got up and walked away. On her way past the bar, she stopped and said something to Luke, who glanced at Meg. Embarrassed to be caught eavesdropping, Meg turned and looked out the window.

She caught her breath.

There he was outside—the same man she'd seen at the library. He stood beneath a tree, looking even more mysterious in the shadows. She recognized him on a gut level—those same dark eyes and sullen attitude. Their eyes met for a heart-stopping moment, and she knew him in a way she couldn't explain. Not his name or how he fit into her life, but she knew his essence, the way his body molded perfectly against her own, the sound of his voice in the heat of the night.

He tipped his head, cupped his hand around a lighter, and lit a cigarette. She should have found it unattractive, but instead he made it look incredibly sexy, like those old movies with rebels like James Dean, who always had a cigarette dangling from sensuous lips and a smoldering scowl on their face. He leaned casually against the tree, epitomizing a time when smoking was cool and bad boys were hot.

Sierra came back to the bar and waved a hand in front of Meg's face. "Hey, everything okay?"

Meg blinked, then forced a smile. "Yes. I was just daydreaming, that's all." For some reason, she didn't want to share this secret with Sierra. Even though it was just a feeling and not a real memory, it was something she had that was all her own, not filtered through someone else's experience.

She took another long swallow and wondered if the beer had anything to do with the way she was feeling. But no, she hadn't even finished half a glass. She couldn't be that much of a lightweight drinker.

She had her back to the door when it opened, but she knew he'd come in. She felt it in the air. It was charged with electricity, the way it feels when a storm is about to release its fury.

Heavy steps drew closer. She focused on each one. Every nerve in her body vibrated. Her heartbeat accelerated until she felt as if it would escape from her chest. All the while, questions assaulted her brain. Who was he? Why did he feel so familiar? What did he want from her?

Meg held her breath and waited for a touch, a word. But he walked right by her without looking back, and she was strangely disappointed. She turned to Sierra. "Do you know that man?"

Sierra shook her head. "No. Why?"

"No reason. Just thought he looked familiar, that's all."

Sierra frowned, a worried expression on her face.

Their burgers came, but Meg's appetite had disappeared. She made a show of eating, but her attention wasn't on her food. It was connected to the dark-haired man, like some kind of strange, psychic umbilical cord. She dared not look in his direction, afraid she'd catch him staring at her with unspoken knowledge.

She caught movement from the side of her vision and turned to watch. Her eyes knew just where to find him—at the corner table facing front. He looked up and their gaze connected like a lock slipping into place, filling her with a deep, unsettled yearning. How could she know she missed him when she didn't even know who he was?

The man got up and spoke to someone in the band. He took his seat again and stared unblinking in her direction. She couldn't look away.

And then it happened.

The band started playing a song she recognized on a gut level. She was flooded with emotions. Her face flushed and her body heated up, melting like liquid gold.

"What," she choked out. "What's that song?"

"Hmm?" Sierra gave her a strange look. "Boyz II Men, I think. *I'll Make Love To You*. Something like that."

"Lucy said I liked boy bands." The words came out like cotton candy, airy and fragile. They were deceptive, camouflaging emotions that roiled and burned.

She closed her eyes and imagined rough hands on her bare skin, hungry kisses along the nape of her neck. As quickly as it came, the memory melted away like butter on a summer sidewalk. When she opened her eyes, the man was staring straight at her, as if reading her thoughts. She felt an immediate jolt of heat and couldn't look away. He stood and started walking toward her. The closer he got, the hotter she felt.

If he asked her to dance, she wouldn't say no. If he took her hand, she wouldn't pull away. If he wanted her to run away with him, she would.

He placed one booted foot on the chair beside her and leaned on his bent knee, close enough to be intimate, but not too close to feel threatening. His smile held her captive, making her feel as if she'd done something wicked. Or would if she didn't break the spell he had over her. When he spoke, his voice was everything she might have imagined, soft and bluesy, as if it just needed a bass guitar to be complete. "Hey, Ruby."

Her body responded before her brain could make

sense of it. She felt a spark, a tingle, a molten heat. "You must have me confused with someone else," she said, but her voice was shaky. "My name is Meg."

He tipped his head and smiled. "My mistake."

Then he walked away and the lights in the room seemed to dim. She was tempted to call him back, to see the hunger in his eyes one more time. But that was crazy. She was a married woman and he...he was a stranger.

Wasn't he?

Sierra gave her a suspicious look. "Are you sure you don't know him?"

"No." Meg chewed her lower lip. "I mean. I don't know. Something about him seems familiar in a way I can't explain."

He'd called her Ruby, which was wrong but somehow felt very right.

"I'm ready to leave now," Meg said.

Sierra motioned to Luke for the bill while Meg used every ounce of control she had not to look in the man's direction. They paid the bill, gathered their things, and left.

Meg never looked back.

****

Sierra pulled up to the house. Meg tried to think of it as home, but there were no emotions attached to the word. It was just a house. A house that could belong to anyone.

Ben was sitting in the living room when she walked in, so intent on the laptop's screen that he didn't notice she was there.

"You're writing?" she asked.

He looked up and smiled. It was a nice smile. A

sweet smile. A nothing-to-write-home-about smile. "Did you have a good day?"

She set her shopping bags down. "I did. We shopped for clothes, books, and stopped for some crazy hamburger that had a fried egg on top. All in all, a good day."

Ben tapped a few keys, then closed the laptop. "That outfit looks nice on you." He stood up and closed the distance between them. "Goes nice with your hair." He ran his fingers through her hair, combing downward with long, gentle strokes. "I've always loved your hair," he said. "You know it was the first thing that attracted me."

Meg stepped away. "I'm tired. It's been a long day." She yawned. "I think I'm going to turn in, if you don't mind."

Ben looked down, then nodded and forced a smile. "Sure. Sleep well. I'll see you in the morning."

Meg thought she probably should kiss him goodnight. A nice kiss. Not too intimate. The kind of goodnight kiss married couples share. But then the moment passed.

Chapter Twenty

Eighteen Years Ago - St. Ophelia's Home for Girls

Meg sat alone—her sandwich unwrapped, her milk carton unopened, and her apple untouched. She wiped a tear from her eye with an angry swipe.

Gemma plopped down beside her. "Lucy still mad at you, huh?"

"I'm mad at *her*," Meg countered.

"So, you're mad at each other, then."

"Right." Meg kicked a cloud of dirt with the toe of her sneaker. She could hear the sound of laughter through the open window. Lucy was probably having a great time, while Meg sat alone outside.

They'd argued over breakfast. Lucy had said horrible things about Gemma, and Meg had called her jealous and possessive.

"I'm not jealous of *Gemma*," Lucy said with a sneer. "God, give me a break!"

"Then why would you say such things about her?"

Lucy just rolled her eyes. "I give up. I'm going outside. Are you coming or not?"

"I can't," Meg had said. "I have stuff to do."

"Yeah? Like sitting in the corner writing in your journal about how sad and pathetic your life is?"

Meg's anger turned to fury. "Have you been reading my journal? That's private."

"Well, if it's so private, then don't leave it out on your bed for the whole world to read."

Meg pounded her fist on the table, knocking over Lucy's orange juice. The entire glass spilled all over Lucy's school uniform. She'd stomped away to change, and they hadn't spoken since.

"Some best friend she turned out to be."

Gemma nodded. "I hate her, too."

Megan rolled her eyes. "I didn't say I *hated* her." She sniffed. "I'm just mad at her, that's all."

"Well, mad can turn to hate real quick, if someone doesn't do something about it."

"Are you saying I should apologize?"

Gemma sat silently.

"Well, I'm not."

"That's fine, too," Gemma said. "You can sit out here pouting and being sad if that's your choice."

"Just go away," Meg said, wiping a tear from her eyes. "You're no help at all." She pulled her knees up and rested her forehead on them, letting the tears flow. Why did everyone she loved leave? What was wrong with her?

After a while, she looked up to see Lucy standing in front of her with that familiar lopsided grin on her face. "Are you done now?"

Meg shrugged. "I guess."

Lucy reached out her hand and helped Meg to her feet. "I didn't read your stupid journal, you know. But anyone could have. You left it open on the bed."

Meg nodded. "I'm sorry I spilled orange juice all over you. I thought you didn't want to be friends anymore."

Lucy shook her head. "We're blood sisters, silly

goose."

"Best friends forever."

"That's right." Lucy wrapped an arm around Meg's shoulders. "You're stuck with me. Like it or not."

Meg had to hold onto that. They weren't just friends; they were survivors and the keeper of each other's secrets.

Chapter Twenty-One

Present Day

Meg had a brief moment of regret over her impulsive decision. She wasn't sure what made her do it. Maybe she just needed to rebel. Or maybe it was Ben's comment the night before that her hair was the first thing he was attracted to.

She held up the mirror the beautician handed her so she could see the back. It was sleek and styled, short on the back and sides, with a bit of wildness and curl on top. It made her feel more independent, more like a woman than a girl. A woman in charge of her own life.

"I love it," she said.

The beautician smiled back at her reflection. "It suits you."

Meg looked down at the mounds of hair on the floor. It was like shedding her past and embracing the new person she was becoming. She felt lighter, taller, and in control. At least as far as her own hair. Now to take control of the rest of her life.

She stopped at the reception desk to pay, and the woman there handed her a note. "Someone dropped this off for you."

Meg unfolded the note. "Meet me at the park. I'll be waiting at your favorite bench."

Oh, it must be Gemma, she thought. Meg paid her

bill and walked out. The park was only a short walk from the beauty salon. She looked forward to talking to Gemma again. There were so many things she wanted to ask, beginning with that man she'd seen the night before. Surely Gemma would tell her everything she needed to remember about him.

But it wasn't Gemma waiting on the bench. It was *him*. She should have been frightened. After all, he'd been stalking her for two days...perhaps even longer. What did he want?

She almost turned and walked away, but the way he was sitting there, calmly expecting her to show up, changed her mind. Besides, he knew that this was her favorite bench. *She* hadn't even known that until Gemma told her. That meant he knew her as well, and that was a lead she had to follow.

She'd taken on this new role when she'd cut her hair—brave, strong, and independent. Now was her chance to prove it to herself.

She walked up to the bench, ignoring the quivering in her chest. When he turned, his eyes lit up, as if he'd waited a lifetime to see her. "I knew you'd come," he said.

His voice was like a lost memory. "Oh? And why is that?"

"We're connected, you and me."

Her breath escaped in a single sigh. She felt it as well but refused to admit it. "Obviously, you know me," she said. "I'm afraid I can't say the same about you. I had an accident and lost my memory, so you'll have to help me remember."

"That's why I'm here." He patted the bench beside him.

Meg sat down, keeping enough distance between them that the casual observer would simply see two friends having an innocent chat. It didn't feel innocent, however. It felt like a deep, dark secret.

He tipped his head and studied her new haircut. "I like it," he said with a nod. "It's sassy. Like you." He chuckled, and the sound was soft and inviting, like water rippling over smooth rocks, rising and falling with ease.

She couldn't help but smile back. "I'm Meg." She held out her hand, inviting him to do the same.

He clasped her hand and rubbed his thumb over the back of her knuckles in a brief caress. "I'm Clay."

Good. He had a name. She tugged her hand from his and placed it on her lap. "How do I know you?"

His response was shocking and direct. "We're lovers."

She should have been surprised, but she'd known from the moment she'd first laid eyes on him that they were more than friends. Some memories were stored in the mind, while others lived in the soul.

A part of her was disappointed, however. Maybe her feelings for Ben weren't as passionate as they should be, but was cheating on him the answer? "I don't remember."

"Nothing?"

"No." She shook her head. "All I know about my life is what they've told me. Ben, Lucy and Sierra."

Clay frowned. "Who's Sierra?"

"My sister. She was with me last night at the pub, remember?"

Ben took her hand again. "Meg, you don't have a sister named Sierra. You have a sister, but her name is

June, and you haven't seen her since you were eight years old."

"What? No." Meg shook her head. "Sierra is my sister. She came with my parents to the hospital to see me. Ben and Lucy…"

"Ben and Lucy are lying to you. You've been estranged from your parents since you were a child. They accused you of hurting your little sister and trying to kidnap her. They left you in St. Ophelia's Home for Girls and never came back for you. Your family abandoned you, Meg."

"No." Meg covered her ears, trying to block out Clay's words. "No, no, no. That's not true. Why are you saying these things?"

Clay reached for her, but she pulled away. "You're lying," she cried. It couldn't be true. She'd had a perfect life with loving parents and a sister she adored. Why would he say such things?

But as hard as she tried to deny it, a vision struck. Blood—not on a cradle, but a crib—and the feeling of shame and fear that came with it. Could there be some truth to what he was saying? Had she hurt her baby sister and been abandoned because of it?

A voice in her head told her not to listen, to push it away. Meg jumped up and ran, ignoring Clay's cries for her to come back. She ran all the way home and barricaded herself in the house where nothing could hurt her, and painful memories didn't exist.

****

Ben was setting his lunch on one of the outdoor picnic tables on campus when Lucy spotted him. He waved her over. "Hey Lucy, come join me."

She settled across from him. "I was hoping I'd

catch you on your lunch break."

Ben unwrapped a sandwich and offered Lucy half.

"No thanks. I'm not hungry."

"So, what's up?"

Lucy took a deep breath, then let it out with a sigh. "I called Meg this morning and asked if she wanted to join me for lunch. She said no."

"Oh? Maybe she has lunch plans with Sierra? They went out last night."

Lucy felt a flash of jealousy. Sierra didn't even know the real Meg, not really. She didn't know her the way Lucy did, and yet she'd taken her place in Meg's life.

Lucy waved a hand, as if to brush away her resentment. "Meg acted strange. Like she was mad at me or something. Why would she be upset with me?"

"I have no idea," Ben said. "She seemed fine last night."

Lucy felt a swirl of emotions. She wanted her old friend back. She missed Meg. And she missed the part of herself that lived in Meg's memories. In that way, she was a victim of Meg's amnesia as well. "You don't think Sierra is telling her lies about me, do you? I mean, she just makes stuff up on a whim. Who knows what might come out of her mouth."

"Well, let's find out," Ben said. He reached for his phone and shot a quick text to Sierra. "I'm pretty sure she doesn't have a class right now," he said. "Sometimes we meet here to share notes so we can keep our stories straight where Meg is concerned."

Lucy wondered if that wasn't just an excuse for Sierra to spend time with Ben. He must be blind not to notice that Sierra had a crush on him. She thought maybe this whole charade was simply an excuse for Sierra to get closer to Ben. She'd seen the way the girl looked at him, with hero worship shining from her eyes. It put all of Lucy's protective instincts on alert. She couldn't help but worry that it was dangerous to give Sierra total access to Meg.

Ben reached out and covered Lucy's hand with his own. "I do understand," he said. "Sometimes I feel like I'm walking on eggshells, afraid to say the wrong thing and not even knowing what the right thing is."

He wiped a hand across his forehead. "I don't know how to make my wife fall in love with me. I don't even think she likes me, to be honest. She asks me a question, and I have to try to remember which is the right answer—the real one or the one we've made up. She gets this faraway look in her eyes, and I wonder what she's thinking about. Is she beginning to remember? What will happen if she does?"

Lucy felt guilty for thinking only of herself. Of course, this was hard on Ben, too. She wanted to say something encouraging, but nothing came to mind, so the silence stretched out between them. It was only broken when Sierra joined them and took a seat. "Good, I'm glad you're both here. I wanted to fill you in on last night."

Sierra told them about the mistake she'd made the night before calling Luke "her" cousin, then having to correct herself. Ben pulled out a notebook and wrote: *Luke, cousin, Ship's Pub.*

"So, while we were in the bookstore," Sierra continued, "I called Luke and filled him in so he'd play along. Turns out I was standing in the self-help section and found this book." She handed a book to Ben titled,

Change Your Story, Change Your Life.

"See," she said. "There's psychological data to support what we're doing for Meg. She turned to a page she'd flagged and read. "If you want to change your life, then change your story. "

Ben took the book and flipped through some pages. "Mind if I read this?"

"Nope, that's why I bought it. I know you've been feeling guilty, but you don't have to. Everything you're doing, you're doing for the right reasons."

Lucy chimed in. "Did anything else happen last night? Meg was acting strange when I called her today. She seemed upset."

Sierra frowned. "No, not that I can think of. We did see a man at the pub she kept asking me about. Wanted to know if he looked familiar to me. But he called her Ruby, so he must have confused her with someone else."

Lucy's stomach dropped and she felt the blood rush from her cheeks.

"Someone you know?" Ben asked.

Clay, dammit! Lucy shook her head. "No, it just seems odd, that's all."

Ben gave her a suspicious look. She should tell him about Clay, tell him everything. But she'd made a promise to Meg to keep her secrets. Maybe Meg didn't remember asking her, but that didn't mean Lucy was going to break her promise now. The less Ben knew about Clay, the better for all of them.

Lucy stayed with Ben after Sierra left for her next class. She glanced at the book Sierra had left behind. "You know what the difference is?" she asked.

"What?"

"The difference is that in this self-help book, they advise the reader to make the decision to rewrite their own past. It's a *conscious* choice, not a lie forced on them by another, however well-meaning it may be."

Ben looked away. Lucy could see that he wondered the same thing but admitting it to himself would bring the entire wall of lies crumbling down.

"She's different, Luce. It's like this dark cloud has lifted and she's happier. I worry that telling her the truth would bring up all those old memories...the ones that sent her hurtling toward that tree in the first place."

"Oh, Ben. We don't even know if she tried to commit suicide or if it was just an accident."

"But what if it *was* a suicide attempt? What if telling her about her past will cause her to try again?" Ben shook his head. "I never told you about the argument we had that night. I brought home a cradle to surprise her, thinking she was finally pregnant after trying all these months. Then..." he stopped and squeezed his eyes shut, as if trying to block out the memory. "Then I found her birth control pills. We had a huge argument and she stormed out."

Lucy reached across and squeezed his hand.

"What happened that night. It's all my fault."

"No, Ben. It's not." Maybe she couldn't tell Ben about Clay, but she could tell him some things about Meg's past. It might ease his guilt if she told him one of the dark secrets that haunted Meg, something she was sure Meg hadn't shared with Ben.

"Ben, remember I told you Meg had been dropped off at St. Ophelia's a number of times?"

When he nodded, Lucy continued. "Well, when Meg was seven or eight years old, they brought her back for the last time. I don't know exactly what happened, but it was bad. There were rumors that Meg had tried to kill her baby sister. Or hurt her in some way. I don't know the details. We were just kids, and you know how rumors spread. I do know that Meg's parents left her at St. Ophelia's after that and never came back for her."

Ben shook his head. "Meg never told me any of this."

"I know," Lucy said. "It's something she's kept locked up tight inside of her. Meg never talked about it. No one talked about it. But whatever happened that night changed her in ways you and I can't imagine. All of it—her feelings of shame, guilt, and abandonment—can be traced back to that night." She gave Ben's hand a squeeze. "So whatever argument the two of you had was just a trigger, not the cause."

Ben twisted the remains of his lunch bag into a tight ball. "Do you think that's why she lied about taking birth control pills while claiming she wanted to have a baby?"

Lucy knew there was more to it than that, but it wasn't something she could share with Ben. It was up to Meg to share that part of her life if and when her memories returned.

"Yes, I think so," she said, more to help Ben get over his feelings of guilt. She could see this had taken its toll on him as well. But at least he had something to gain by continuing this charade—he had a happy wife, he was writing again, even if it was a fictional account of a woman who didn't exist, and he had people like Sierra telling him it was okay to build this web of lies around his wife.

But Lucy had lost her best friend and she missed her dearly. She missed being able to talk about memories they shared. She missed being the one person Meg could always trust, the friend she could lean on and talk to about her deepest secrets.

Starting with Clay. She wasn't sure what his game was, but if he was following Meg, it couldn't be good.

Chapter Twenty-Two

The first thing Ben noticed when he walked in the door was Meg's hair. She'd chopped it all off. He opened his mouth to ask why, then closed it again. Whatever her reasons, it wasn't worth upsetting her over. But it broke his heart.

When he thought of Meg, the first thing that came to mind was her hair. The clean, floral smell of it, how it shimmered in the sunlight, the feel of it sliding in a soft fall through his fingers. He already missed that swingy ponytail that swayed in time with her hips when she walked, and most of all, the way it spread across his pillow after lovemaking.

Not like that was happening any time soon.

Oh, but her glorious hair. Gone. All gone. Just like the old Meg, the woman he married. In her place was a stranger who pulled away when he reached for her, a stranger who avoided his gaze. The old Meg may have had fits of depression, but she was alive. They fought and made up. Perhaps their sex life wasn't the most wild and passionate, but they had a connection that was strong and sweet.

"I love you, Meg." They were the first words that came out of his mouth.

She looked at him and smiled.

"Your hair. It looks...cute."

She ran her hand through the short curls, as if just

remembering she'd cut it all off.

"Hey," he said, dropping his briefcase on the counter and perching on one of the bar stools. "I have an idea. Why don't we go out to tonight to celebrate the new you." Oh damn, that hadn't come out right. "I mean your new haircut."

She tipped her head and gave him a calculating smile. "My cousin Luke's place?"

Ben frowned...glad Sierra had filled him in today. "The Ship's Pub? Nah, I was thinking some place a little more elegant."

Meg walked over to the coffee maker and lifted the coffee pot with a questioning glance in Ben's direction. When he nodded, she poured them each a cup and carried them to the counter.

Ben had a moment of indecision. Should he just drink it black the way she'd brought it to him or admit that he used cream in his coffee and make her feel bad for not knowing something as simple as how her own husband takes his coffee.

Not a big deal, he thought, standing up and casually walking to the refrigerator for the cream. He poured it in his coffee as if it didn't matter at all that she didn't know. There were already too many lies to keep track of. This was just one less lie to worry about.

Meg took a sip of her coffee—black, the way she liked it. "Let me ask you a question."

"What's that?"

"What kind of elegant place would I normally choose to go to for dinner?" Her smile reminded him of the old Meg.

"Well, there are a few options." He counted them off on his fingers. "There's the Lanyard, which makes an incredible prime rib dinner. You always end up taking half of it home and making roast beef sandwiches with the leftovers. Then there's Milano's Italian Restaurant, which has the best lasagna this side of Italy. Not to mention homemade cannoli."

Ben smiled, remembering the last time they'd gone there. They'd brought home half a dozen cannolis and eaten them in bed, making a sticky mess of the sheets and each other with sweet cream and chocolate.

"What?" she asked.

He shook his head. "Nothing. Just remembering how much you love their cannoli."

She nodded her head. "Then Milano's it is."

****

So far Ben was doing okay. She'd tested him about Luke's pub and pretended she didn't know he took cream in his coffee. Both times he'd passed the test.

And he was right about the lasagna. It was delicious. Ben looked appealing in the soft candlelight. Maybe the two glasses of Chianti had something to do with that. She felt an appreciation for all he'd been through. It couldn't be easy having a wife who couldn't remember falling in love with you, or the day you proposed, or moving into your first apartment.

It couldn't be easy at all.

"Okay, twenty questions," she said. "I'm trying to learn more about my life before concussion."

He snorted. "Okay, go ahead."

"Where did we meet?"

"A little sports bar called Cappy's. It's still around. As a matter of fact, it's near the hospital. I stopped by there more than a few times for a bite to eat." He stopped and smiled. "You were a waitress there. You had this cute little ponytail that..." He stopped and glanced at her hair, then looked away. "Next question?"

She decided it was best not to get into the hair issue. Suddenly her impulsive decision to cut it off seemed more like a child's tantrum. Easier to change the subject. "How did I get into the cupcake business?"

"Well, that's a funny story. You volunteered to make cupcakes for a church potluck and couldn't decide what kind to make, so..."

Meg had tuned him out from the moment he'd said church. She belonged to a church? Which one? What were her beliefs? But Ben was on a roll, and she didn't want to interrupt. She made a mental note to ask him later.

"...so, you searched through all of your cookbooks and pulled out about a dozen recipes and spent the next two weeks trying a different one each day. I think I gained ten pounds taste testing, and in the end, you still couldn't decide which one to bring to the potluck. So you brought three different kinds, and everyone raved about them. I can't remember who told you that you should go into the cupcake business, but the idea stuck."

He shook his head and laughed. "Then you ran it by your sidekick."

"Lucy?"

"Right. And before you could say 'sprinkles,' she'd picked up an old food truck, and the two of you painted and decorated it, made signs, and menus and...bang, Lucy quit her job, and the two of you were in business."

"Sweet Sensations."

"That's right." He reached across the table and squeezed her hand. "I didn't think you guys would last two months, but you surprised me. You have a great little business going. Your clients are anxiously awaiting your return."

Meg felt a strange sense of pride. She didn't need a memory to follow a recipe. Maybe it was time she and Lucy got back on the road. Another thought to file away for another time. Just not tonight.

"What's my maiden name?"

"Why...?" Ben gave a small shake of his head. "It's Anderson."

Bingo. That was the information she needed to begin digging into her past. She raised her empty glass. "I think I'll have another."

"Are you sure?" Ben asked. "Two is usually your limit. After three..." He stopped, a blush climbing to his cheeks.

"What happens after three?"

"You get, um...amorous." He tipped his head and raised his eyebrows with a knowing glance. He looked adorable in a puppy-like kind of way.

Meg raised her glass when the server came by. "One more," she said with a flirty smile.

Perhaps this was the answer to finding her way back to her past. She may not remember the ceremony, but Ben was her husband and he'd been through a lot. Maybe together they could find their way back to some semblance of a marriage.

****

Ben couldn't remember the last time they'd had such an enjoyable evening. It made him realize how much Meg's depression had cast a pall over their lives in the recent years.

Tonight reminded him of the old days when they'd

enjoyed just being together. Meg was playful, flirtatious. She reached out and stroked the back of his wrist. He turned his hand over and clasped hers, then brought it to his lips and brushed them across her knuckles. She cast her eyes downward, then back again.

"I love you, Meg." The words came out easily and automatically. He knew she couldn't say it in return because she didn't remember loving him. But the yearning in her eyes told him she wanted to, and he was determined to do everything in his power to make her fall in love with him again.

On the way home she rested her head on his shoulder. Her breathing was soft and easy. When she spoke, it came as a shock. "I saw a cradle in the basement," she said.

He held his breath. Did she remember the argument?

"Are we…were we trying to have a baby?"

Ben wasn't sure how to answer that. "Yes," he said. For him, at least, that was the truth. "We've been trying for months."

She nodded. The silence lasted moments, then she replied with a soft, wistful sigh. "Maybe we should continue trying."

She trailed a fingertip along his inner thigh, sending shockwaves to his groin. He had all he could do not to pull the car over and take her right then and there. But no, he had to go slow. She had to feel safe in his arms.

Once inside, he seduced her with wine and chocolate and slow, sweet kisses. He knew every inch of her body, the way she liked to be touched and the places where his lips would make her melt. It gave him an unfair advantage because she didn't know he knew her body so well, but it was an advantage he was willing to take if it meant getting his wife back in his bed.

For Meg, letting go had always been the biggest hurdle to overcome. She'd always fought losing control, even when it came to sex. This time, however, Ben could sense the moment she gave in and allowed herself to be swept away. She didn't struggle or hold back but went with the flow as easily as the sand is swept away by the tide.

She gave as well as took, letting him know that she wanted this as much as he did. When she came, it was with complete abandon, rather than fearful surrender. He hadn't realized how much had been missing from their sex life, and now that he knew, he never wanted to go back.

Afterward, Ben cradled Meg in his arms. He smiled at the soft, purring sounds she made as she drifted off. His heart felt as if it would burst with love for this woman, his wife.

He felt a twinge of guilt over the fact that they'd had unprotected sex, but she hadn't been taking birth control pills since the accident, so taking one tonight wouldn't have made any difference. Besides, how would he explain it to her since he'd just told her they'd been trying to conceive? And since they'd been trying to have a baby, or so he thought, he didn't have condoms in the house. Besides, they'd been caught up in the moment. The last thing on his mind had been one more deception.

He kept reminding himself that it was all for Meg's own good. When was the last time she'd slept this peacefully? It made all the lies worthwhile.

Chapter Twenty-Three

Every time Ben glanced her way, Meg felt herself blush. He was her husband, but he was still a stranger. A stranger she'd shared a bed with last night.

She wanted to be intimate with Ben, to accept him completely as her husband. But the things Clay had said still weighed on her mind. Who should she trust? The man she'd married, or the one who claimed to be her soul mate and lover. Even though she had no memory of her past, Meg didn't feel like she was the kind of woman who'd cheat on her husband. But the attraction to Clay was undeniable.

She was relieved when Ben finally left for work so she could continue trying to find clues to her past without him following her around with love-struck, puppy dog eyes. She wanted to trust him, but the seeds of doubt had taken root and Meg worried that she couldn't trust anyone—not Ben, not Lucy or Sierra, and not Clay.

Hours later, the house was a mess. She'd torn apart closets, emptied drawers and searched high and low for something she could hold onto—a tiny piece of truth that would reveal the lies.

But nothing was to be found.

She'd emptied out her jewelry box, not surprised to find dozens of pieces of semi-precious jewelry. Nothing ostentatious, but not exactly dime-store trinkets. There were some nice rings and bracelets, which she probably paired with equally mediocre clothes. Whoever Meg was—or had been—seemed to feel it was more important to fit in than to be her own unique self.

When Meg replaced the jewelry, the felt organizer shifted a bit. Only then did she notice it was seated inside the box. She grasped one of the sections between two fingers and pulled. The insert lifted easily, revealing another compartment below.

Inside was a beautiful jeweled, dragonfly pin. Meg lifted it up and studied it. The sun hit the wings, making them shimmer. It felt as if the dragonfly could take wing and lift off into the sky. There was something familiar about the pin. Had she seen it in a dream or vision? Why was it hidden in the bottom of her jewelry box?

She caught a wisp of memory—snowdrifts, a shimmering dragonfly and Gemma. It felt distant and dreamy, like the memory of a memory of a memory. She could hear Gemma's voice, clear as crystal. "There are answers to be found if you're ready to hear them. Trust the dragonfly. It will lead you to the truth. All you have to do is follow."

Meg wasn't sure exactly what that meant, but it felt right and true. Her hands shook as she pinned the dragonfly to her collar. Also, inside the lower compartment was a stiff and yellowed newspaper clipping. Meg's heart skipped a beat when she read the headline: *St. Ophelia's Home for Girls Celebrates Twenty-Five Year Anniversary.*

There was a picture with the article. A dozen young girls all wearing the same maroon jumpers over crisp white blouses lined up with camera-ready smiles that failed to reach their eyes. Meg recognized Lucy right away, the same curly red hair and bright smile. She had one arm thrown around another young girl who might have been trying to hide in the background.

Is that me?

Meg studied the picture. Of course, it was, but how sad and forlorn that child looked. She looked nothing like the picture Sierra and Ben had painted of a happy, carefree child growing up in modest surroundings with a loving family. The child in this picture was shrouded in hopelessness. Instead of looking directly at the camera, her eyes were on her friend, her expression unreadable. Meg's heart went out to her younger self. *What happened to you? Why can't I remember?*

As she scanned the picture, something else caught her eye. There was a woman standing with the children. A woman not much older than Meg was now, wearing a navy cardigan over a ruffled blouse as white as snow. She had a kind face and gentle smile. But it wasn't the woman's face that caught Meg's attention. It was the dragonfly pin at her collar, resting at an angle as if ready to take flight. It was the same pin Meg had found tucked away at the bottom of her jewelry box.

She unclipped the pin and stared at it. Yes, it was definitely the same one. A feeling of guilt and shame came over her. Had she stolen the pin from this kind woman? Had that sad, hopeless child taken something that didn't belong to her in order to feel worthwhile? The thought made her so sad. She thought of all the jewelry in the box. Was that little girl still trying to find meaning and a sense of self-worth in material objects?

She ran her finger along the names below the picture, stopping at the woman's name—Carly Shay.

She knew the pin in the picture was the same one she held in her hand, sparkling with the colors of the sea. She'd return the pin to its rightful owner and apologize for that sad little girl who had nothing to call her own.

Meg slipped the pin back into the hidden compartment. She had to stop herself from thinking about the girl as someone separate. That girl was part of the past she couldn't remember. A past that included being left alone in a place for abandoned children.

So, Clay was right? Not that it mattered. Just because he was right about one thing didn't necessarily mean everything he'd said was true.

Meg reached for her cell phone and looked up information about St. Ophelia's Home for Girls. Once she had a phone number, it took her a few minutes to work up the courage to make the phone call.

When the call was answered, her brain went blank. She should have rehearsed what she wanted to say. "Hi. My name is Meg. Meg Tyler." No, that wasn't right. What had Ben said her maiden name was? "Anderson," she corrected. "Meg Anderson."

She shook her head and tried again. "I've had an accident and lost my memory. I think I was once a..." A what? *Student, ward, prisoner*? "I think I once lived there, but..."

"I'm sorry," the calmly efficient voice on the other end interrupted. "We can't give out any personal information over the telephone. If you'd like to speak to someone personally, I could set up an appointment for early next week."

Meg started to argue, then realized that Ben would be home soon, and the weekend was coming up. She didn't want to have to answer questions about where she was going and why. It would be easier to slip away unnoticed during the week while he was at school. That being the case, she made an appointment for the following Monday, hoping that she could uncover enough information between now and then to make finding her records easier.

After disconnecting, she looked at the picture again. The two girls leaned toward each other, speaking volumes about how close they were. Meg could clearly see Lucy's features in the face of the child in the picture. Her chin pushed out defiantly, her arm closed protectively around the other girl in the picture.

Meg refused to think of the child as herself. She didn't feel any empathy for that lost little girl avoiding the camera's unblinking eye. That girl wasn't even a memory. She was the ghost of someone Meg didn't know.

She tucked the mementos back in the jewelry box and put it away, then went to work putting everything back in order so Ben wouldn't know she'd been searching for proof of his lies.

But she knew. And if he'd lied about St. Ophelia's, then what else had he lied about? He'd taken her into his bed under false pretenses.

She wouldn't make that mistake again.

****

Once the house was back in order, Meg made a pitcher of lemonade and took it out to the front porch. It was a beautiful spring day with a gentle breeze that carried with it the scent of lilacs. She set the lemonade and two glasses on a table and sat in a white wicker chair to wait for Ben so they could talk about the things she'd discovered about her past.

Everything inside told her that Ben had to have a good reason for lying to her. She struggled to understand. If Lucy and Ben were lying, did it mean Clay was telling the truth? Had she been cheating on Ben with another man?

Lucy would know. Lucy knew all of her secrets. For the first time, Meg was afraid of what she might find out about the woman she was before the accident. Maybe there were other people who could shed some light on her past.

A movement caught her eye and she glanced up. Gemma was standing by the side of the porch. "Come on up," Meg said. "Would you like a glass of lemonade?"

Gemma climbed up the porch steps and took a seat on a white wicker chair across from Meg. "No thanks."

"I was just thinking of you," Meg said. "Well, I was wondering about anyone I knew besides Lucy growing up. I just found out I spent time at St. Ophelia's. Were you there, too?"

Gemma nodded her head and smiled. "Yes, we were both there."

"What do you remember about me?"

"I remember a lot. What do you remember?"

"Nothing," Meg said. "I don't even remember being there. If I hadn't found an old newspaper article, I wouldn't have believed it myself."

"The mind is a funny thing," Gemma said. "Sometimes it tries to protect us from ourselves." She tipped her head and smiled. "When you're ready, you'll remember it all."

"Maybe. But it's hard. You don't know what it's like not knowing who you really are."

"Oh, but you *do* know who you are," Gemma replied. "Maybe you can't remember the experiences that changed you, but you always know, deep down in your soul, who you are. And that, my dear, is all that matters in the end."

Meg smiled, remembering their shared joke. "And if it's not okay..."

"It's not the end," Gemma finished.

Meg didn't remember Gemma leaving. One moment they were chatting like old friends and the next Ben was shaking her awake. "Hey, sleepyhead. Have you been out here long?"

Meg rubbed the sleep from her eyes. She glanced at her watch. It had only been an hour since she'd first come out, but she felt as if she'd been asleep all day. It wasn't like her to nap, or at least she didn't think so. She blamed the soft breeze and summer sunshine for lulling her to sleep.

"I was hoping we could talk." She pointed to the pitcher of lemonade and waited while Ben poured himself a glass. There was no sense beating around the bush. "I found a newspaper clipping today. It shows me and Lucy at a home for girls."

She waited, but Ben was silent. "Why didn't you tell me?" she asked.

He leaned back, took a deep breath and let it out with a sigh. "After your accident, the doctors said we should try not to upset you."

When it seemed as if he wasn't going to say more, she prodded. "So then?"

Ben wouldn't meet her gaze. "Then you seemed happy," he said. "I didn't want to risk that."

"Why would knowing my past risk that? I mean, so

I grew up in a home. So did Lucy. I don't see why you'd have to go to the extent of..." A sudden thought struck her, one she'd been trying to avoid thinking about. "Those lovely people. Mabel and Norm. They're not my real parents, are they?"

Ben looked away, guilt turning his face into that of a stranger. He gave a miniscule shake of his head, but that was enough to strike a spear of pain, betrayal, and grief through her heart. "And Sierra?"

"She's one of my students." Ben pushed his glass away, avoiding Meg's gaze. "She looked so much like you that when she offered to play the part of your sister, it seemed...I don't know, it seemed like a good idea at the time."

The truth couldn't have been more painful if Meg had lost an actual sister. Even now, knowing it was all a charade, the loss felt raw and bone deep. She went from having a trusted sibling and loving parents to realizing she was all alone, an orphan abandoned and left to survive on her own.

No, not on her own. She'd had Lucy.

Ben reached for her, but Meg pulled away. She couldn't. His betrayal was a brick wall between them. "What about Lucy? Did she just go along with you?"

"She fought me every step of the way," Ben admitted. "It just snowballed, Meg. I honestly thought I was doing what was best for you. I thought if we could rewrite your past, things would be different."

"Different how?" The cold steel of her voice betrayed the rage burning inside.

"I thought you'd be less depressed," Ben admitted. "Less volatile. Less..." he looked at her with such pain in his eyes that Meg almost forgave him for his lies, but she could tell he was still holding something back. The lies were still trapped between them. He looked away. "Less angry."

"I guess it didn't work," she said. "I'm angry now. More angry than you can imagine." She stood and went inside for her purse and keys. When she returned, Ben was still sitting, shoulders slumped and head bowed.

"I'm leaving, Ben."

"Please, Meg. Let's talk."

She shook her head. "I can't. I don't want to talk. You lied to me, Ben. You betrayed my trust. I don't want to be here anymore."

Ben stood up. "Where will you go?"

"I don't know. Just not here." With that she turned and walked away into a future that was as unknown as her own past.

****

She hadn't been looking for Clay. But maybe she was hoping he'd find her when she went to the Ship's Pub. She felt somehow defiant sitting alone.

Luke came up to the counter, pulled a pencil from behind his ear. "What can I get you?"

She glared at him. "You're not my cousin."

"Sorry, that's not on the menu. "He shot her an impetuous grin. "How about a fish fry? It's tonight's special."

Meg looked away, refusing to be charmed. "I'll have Merlot."

"Two for one tonight."

"Perfect. Start me off with one."

"Look, I'm sorry," he said. "I was just playing along. I didn't know what Sierra was up to, but I figured she didn't mean any harm."

Meg let it drop. She was tired of talking about it, tired of thinking about it, and damn tired of living it. When Luke returned with the wine, she played with the stem of the glass, rocking it back and forth. She really didn't want the drink. She just wanted something to do with her hands to keep them from nervously clenching and unclenching.

She knew the moment Clay walked in the door. The air became denser and the hairs lifted on the back of her arms. One moment she was alone basking in a pool of self-pity, and then she wasn't. He sidled up on the stool beside her, exuding heat and a musky scent that triggered every pheromone and pleasure center in her brain.

"Are you following me?" she asked.

"Yes."

She hadn't expected that. His voice was slow and sexy, the perfect voice for pillow talk. *Stop*, she warned herself. That was dangerous territory.

"You were right," she admitted.

"Yeah?" His gaze was so intense that for a moment she forgot what she was going to say.

"About my parents, the orphanage...everything." Well, not exactly everything. There was no newspaper clipping saying she had a lover, but if Clay was right about some things, he was probably right about all of it. He just may be the only person she could rely on to tell her the truth.

Luke came by and took Clay's order, giving Meg a moment to try to catch her thoughts. One thing she knew for sure about Clay was that she was intensely attracted to him. From the time he sat down she struggled to keep her hands off him. She wanted to touch, pet, caress.

He leaned closer, brushing against the hollow of her cheek, then whispering in her ear. "Now do you believe we're lovers?"

How could she not? Her body was on fire for him. She couldn't help comparing the passion she felt with Clay to the comfortable, but passionless feelings she had for her own husband.

"Let me prove it to you." He left a twenty-dollar bill on the counter, then took her arm and walked her out of the pub without touching the drink he'd ordered.

He took her to another bar, this one dark and smoky, a place that felt secretive. They sat at a table tucked into a corner, lit only by candlelight. The booths were lined in red velour—as soft and sensuous as a lover's caress. With a snap of his fingers, Clay summoned a server. "Black Velvet on the rocks. Two." He turned and winked at Meg. "Make them doubles."

Meg opened her mouth to argue but stopped. Why not? Black Velvet sounded wickedly perfect.

"Do you remember this place?" Clay asked.

Meg shook her head.

Clay looked away and fiddled with a coaster. "This is where you'd sneak away to meet me whenever you could."

Somehow Meg had suspected she wasn't all sweetness and light, as Lucy and Ben would have her believe. She suspected she had a dark side, and the dark side in her was unmistakably drawn to Clay.

When their drinks came, he raised his glass in a salute. His eyes sparkled in the candlelight, hinting of promise. She touched her glass to his and smiled back.

"To us," he said, then downed the amber liquid in

one smooth swallow.

Meg tried to do the same but coughed halfway through. A ribbon of fire burned its way down her throat, pooling heat in her belly, then traveling along her arms and legs. She quickly downed the rest of the whiskey and felt her limbs go loose.

Clay shot her an approving nod. "That's my girl." His words only added more heat to the fire now spreading to her groin. It burned. It burned so good.

He took her hand and led her to a dimly lit dance floor. On stage, a woman with fiery hair and kohl-rimmed eyes sang something slow and throaty. Clay pressed his hand to Meg's lower back and pulled her close. They moved as one—slow and sensuous. His breath was a seductive whisper in her ear, his body hard and hungry against her own.

This was what she'd been missing in her marriage. This passion, this burning desire.

"You may not remember me," Clay said, "but you feel it, don't you? Your body remembers."

"Yes." The word was a sigh.

"Come home with me."

"I can't.

"Make love with me."

Her breath caught in her throat.

"Let me show you who you really are, Meg. Together we'll make new memories. Beautiful memories." He pulled her closer, tighter, his body promising an entire world of passion to explore.

It was a passion she yearned for. She wanted to feel alive, not just a cardboard figure formed from someone else's memory. She wanted to write something new on this blank slate—something as hot as dark whiskey, as erotic as a torch song, and as sensual as lush, red velour.

"Yes," she said. The word escaped without a conscious decision. "Yes."

He brushed her mouth with full, soft lips, then slid his hand to the back of her neck and held her close as his mouth devoured, sweeping away any lingering doubt.

Long into the night they burned in a blaze of sizzling passion.

Chapter Twenty-Four

Lucy had been up all night. She couldn't do this anymore. Meg was her best friend. They'd never lied to one another. She shouldn't have let Ben talk her into going along with his lies.

No more. She was going to come clean and explain to Meg why she'd gone along with this charade. Meg was reasonable. Surely, she'd understand.

Ben answered her knock on the door. His eyes were red rimmed. He looked as if he'd been up all night too. She peeked over his shoulder.

"Meg's not here," he said.

Lucy pushed past him. "Good, because I want to talk to you alone. I think we need to come clean and tell Meg the truth. She'll understand. Yeah, she might be pissed at first, but she's reasonable and…Ben?"

"Someone beat us to it," he said. "She knows we lied to her." He shook his head. "I've never seen her like this before."

"Angry?"

"No. Not angry. Cold. Cold and distant." He lowered his head, but not before Lucy saw a tear roll down his cheek. "I think I've really lost her this time, Luce."

Lucy put her arm around Ben's shoulder. She'd warned him, but that didn't stop her from being sympathetic. "How long has she been gone?"

"All night," he admitted. "I hoped she was with you, but..."

Lucy shook her head. The fact that Meg hadn't come to her stung. "Maybe she's with Sierra?"

"I don't know." Ben reached into his pocket for his phone. "I'll give her a call."

Lucy listened to Ben's side of the conversation with a growing sense of dread. Her fears were confirmed when Ben hung up and related what he'd found out.

"Sierra's cousin said Meg was at the pub with a strange man. Someone who'd come in a few nights earlier when Sierra brought Meg there."

Lucy nodded. She had her suspicions about this *strange* man, and if she was correct, it didn't bode well for Meg. Luckily, she knew right where to find him.

****

With the first rays of the rising sun came regret. Meg felt scorched, empty, and a little used. She was ashamed of her impulsive decision to sleep with Clay. Was this who she was? A cheater? A liar? Was this who she wanted to be?

And yet when Clay slipped out of bed, all sleepy eyed and gloriously naked, she wanted him again, her body at odds with her brain. Her brain won, but just barely.

She was fully dressed when Clay came out of the shower, a towel draped dangerously low on his hips. "Hey what's the hurry? I thought we'd have breakfast in bed and..."

"No." She made a conscious effort not to stare at the towel and what lay beneath it.

He crossed the room and held out his arms, but she

pushed him away. "I have to go home."

His face hardened. "Home?" His smile twisted into a sneer. "To him? After what we shared?"

"I need time to think."

Clay reached out and gripped her upper arms, then gave her a quick shake. It wasn't hard, but the world went still for a moment. In the space between heartbeats, a memory tried to surface. It had no shape, but it reeked of fear.

She wrenched herself free. "Don't." Her voice sounded vulnerable to her ears. "Don't ever…"

But before she could finish the sentence someone pounded on the door. Meg and Clay both turned and stared. The banging continued, along with a voice shouting from the other side. "Meg, are you in there? It's Lucy. Let me in."

At the sound of her friend's voice, Meg rushed to the door and threw it open. Lucy wrapped her arms around her. "I was afraid I'd find you here." She turned and glared at Clay, then back to Meg. "What did he do to you? Did he hurt you?"

"No," Meg said. "He just…" Meg stared at her feet. There was no use lying. It was obvious why she was there. "I came voluntarily. Clay told me everything. How you and Ben lied to me."

Lucy nodded. "I was coming to explain today. I don't want to lie to you anymore."

"So, it's true, right? Everything. St. Ophelia's, my sister, everything?"

"Yes."

"Clay was the only one telling me the truth."

Lucy glared at Clay. "That depends. What exactly did he tell you?"

"He said we were lovers."

"Oh, did he?" Lucy shook her head. "You were. Years ago. When you were teenagers. It was a toxic relationship then, Meg. He nearly destroyed you. Ben's the one who came to your rescue. Ben's the one who put the pieces back together when Clay left you broken and shattered."

Meg glanced at Clay. He looked away.

Lucy tugged on Meg's shoulder. "You're not a cheater, Meg. Maybe you and Ben have issues, but you'd never betray him. That's not who you are. Clay lied to you. You haven't seen him in almost ten years.

Meg felt all the air leave her body. She blinked tears away and turned to Clay. "Is that true?"

He shrugged a shoulder. "So, what if it is? You can't deny what we have. Even after all these years." His smile was smug. Predatory.

Meg wanted to scream. More lies. Was there no one she could trust? She grabbed her purse off the side table and brushed past Lucy on her way out the door.

"Meg."

She held up her hand. "No. No more lies. I can't trust any of you." With that she ran from the people who claimed to be her friends, determined to uncover the truth on her own.

****

After wandering the streets for nearly half an hour, Meg stopped and looked around. She had no idea where she was. She hadn't been paying attention when Clay brought her to his apartment, focused instead on the sexual heat he'd aroused in her. She was in an unfamiliar part of town, with no idea where she would go even if she knew where she was.

She had nearly five hundred dollars in her purse. She'd found it stashed away in an English teapot. She didn't want to think why she'd been hoarding money. Maybe it was just an emergency fund. Or maybe she'd been planning to run away all along.

There were credit cards as well, but they were a last resort. Until Meg knew what she intended to do, she didn't want Ben to track her down. She needed time alone to think, without any distraction.

She stopped in a coffee shop and found a seat, trying to collect her thoughts. What was she going to do? The coffee was bitter and so was her mood. Everything around her was falling apart.

The door opened and a woman walked in. Her stomach was round and heavy, in the last trimester of pregnancy. Meg's heart gave a lurch and a wave of sorrow threatened to overwhelm her. She put her hand to her own stomach. Her body felt hollow inside, her heart numb with grief. She tried to stand, but her knees buckled, and she fell back in her chair. A sense of loss so deep and dark washed over her she felt she'd drown.

As quickly as it came, the feeling faded away. Momentary, but so deep she knew it had to be a memory trying to rise to the surface. A memory that was so painful her subconscious immediately pushed it back down.

Why had she reacted that way? Her hands went to her stomach, expecting…what? Nothing. She was empty inside.

If the buried memories held so much pain, maybe she was better off not knowing. She pushed the coffee aside, left some money on the table, and walked out of the coffee shop, making a conscious effort not to look in the direction of the pregnant woman.

Outside, she wandered the streets. A gentle breeze tossed her hair and cooled her skin. She'd probably walked these streets hundreds of times, but today she felt no recognition. Still, a part of her suspected something familiar would show itself at the next turn.

From the corner of her eye, she caught sight of movement. A woman, hurrying across the street. It looked like...

"Gemma?" Meg cried out, but the woman didn't turn. She hurried forward, then ducked into a doorway. Meg rushed after her, but by the time she was inside, Gemma had disappeared.

"Can I help you?"

Meg blinked and looked around, realizing she was standing in a hotel lobby. A well-dressed woman behind the counter tipped her head expectantly.

"I, um..."

"Would you like a room?"

Meg nodded. Why hadn't she thought of getting a hotel room? If not for the fact that she'd followed a woman who looked like Gemma, she'd still be wandering the streets lost and alone.

"Yes," she said. She paid for two nights with cash. That would get her through the weekend. Monday she'd visit St. Ophelia's, and after that she'd decide what she was going to do.

But where was Gemma when she needed her most? Something in Meg believed that Gemma guarded all the secrets buried inside her snow-covered darkness. She wanted to run from room to room, searching for answers. She'd knock on every door if it meant she would find Gemma and uncover the real truth once and for all.

Instead, she unlocked the door to her own room and stepped inside. It was clean, simple, and devoid of personality. No more familiar than the house she called a home. A clean slate, just like herself. And there was comfort in that. She could imprint this room with her own memories.

There was a hotel notepad and pen on the nightstand. Meg sat and made three columns, listing all the "facts" she'd heard from Ben, Lucy, and Clay. She didn't bother with Sierra, assuming everything she'd said was simply a part she was playing to please Ben.

Meg knew there had to be truth in there somewhere. They couldn't have invented everything. One thing that really bothered her, however, was Clay's account of her childhood in St. Ophelia's. He'd said she had a sister, and there was some mystery involved. There was a ring of truth to that she couldn't discount for some reason.

It also made sense that Lucy and Ben would try to hide that if they were concerned with her mental state. Meg made a new list and at the top of it wrote—FIND MY SISTER.

Now, with a clear goal in mind, Meg felt a renewed sense of purpose. If she could unlock one secret, maybe she could unlock them all.

She felt 100% better than she had a half hour ago. No longer was she weak and vulnerable, being tossed mindlessly in every direction by other people with their own agenda. Renewed, she was now a woman willing to stand strong and independent with a specific goal in mind and with the determination to do what needed to be done.

Chapter Twenty-Five

By Monday, the anger had simmered into a surge of determination. Meg had spent the weekend getting her thoughts in order and practicing what she'd say. She'd made a list of questions to ask so she wouldn't forget anything, and she mentally prepared herself for whatever answers she uncovered.

Meg called for a car and made a cup of hotel coffee while she waited. When it arrived, she gave the driver directions to St. Ophelia's Home for Girls, then sat back and crossed her hands over her nerve-churning stomach.

She purposely arrived early, wanting to absorb as much as she could alone before speaking to the director. She secretly hoped something would jog her memory. If she'd spent most of her childhood at St. Ophelia's. Surely, she'd remember something.

There was nothing special about the building. It was square, brick and nondescript. The grounds were neat, but not professionally landscaped. Lilac bushes grew wild along a chain-link fence surrounding a playground. The smell of lilacs triggered pleasant emotions, but no specific memories.

Girls of all ages filled the yard. Some on the swings, some sitting at tables playing cards, while others giggled in small, intimate groups. They all wore the same uniform—maroon jumpers over crisp white shirts. The girls looked neat, clean, and happy. Meg wasn't sure what she'd expected, maybe some cross between a Charles Dickens novel and Little Orphan Annie. The sound of laughter carried on a lilac-scented breeze was both refreshing and unexpected.

She stepped inside, breathing in a scent that belonged to an unremembered past, a combination of lemons and astringent. It plucked at her memories without revealing anything at all, just a lingering sense of familiarity.

The walls were painted neutral beige. Glossy, no doubt to resist crayons, fingerprints, and peanut butter. St. Ophelia's seemed like a place where children could play unrestrained. Framed pictures graced the walls, each labeled with the year they were taken. Meg found the pictures of her youth through photographs. Many of the faces changed from year to year, but Lucy was always there.

The years progressed, and she saw Lucy and herself grow from children to teenagers—always together, always side-by-side. They had a history and a bond, more like sisters than real siblings, because they only had each other to depend on. So why would Lucy go along with Ben's lies?

Meg shook her head. She couldn't make a decision until she had all the facts. What about Gemma? She went back and searched the pictures for Gemma's face, but there was no sign of her. Hadn't Gemma said she'd been there as well? Why wasn't she in any of the pictures?

Before Meg could search further, her gaze was drawn to a woman in several of the pictures. There was something familiar about her. Then Meg realized why.

It was the same woman she'd seen in the newspaper clipping, and she was wearing the same dragonfly pin on her collar. The pin Meg had found tucked away in a hidden compartment of her jewelry box. Why did Meg have that pin? Had she stolen it from the woman in the picture?

There wasn't time to mull that over. She glanced at her watch and realized it was time to meet the director with the hope of finding some answers. She double-checked the paper she'd tucked in her purse—Mrs. Shay, Room 36.

Meg found the room and knocked on the door. It was opened by a middle-aged woman with fair skin and blonde hair pulled into a neat bun that looked elegantly chic. When she saw Meg, her face lit up and her eyes sparkled.

"Megan!" She pulled Meg into a warm hug. "I'm sorry, I didn't recognize your married name. Why didn't you tell me it was you?"

The woman's obvious surprise only mirrored Meg's own. "You know me?"

"Of course, I do. I don't forget any of my girls. Come, have a seat."

My girls?

Meg entered the room and took a seat in front of Mrs. Shay's desk. On the wall behind her chair were pictures—graduation photos, wedding pictures, a young woman holding an infant. There was something poignant about those picture that made her feel sad. "Are those your children?"

Mrs. Shay nodded and pointed at them with pride. "My daughters, Olivia and Grace. They anchor my heart." She turned back to Meg. "Do you have any children?"

The question was innocent enough, but Meg felt that same sense of pain she'd felt a few days ago seeing the pregnant woman in the coffee shop. Pain, loss, and a fierce sense of betrayal. She shook her head. "No. Not yet."

Mrs. Shays eyes were kind, yet piercing, as if she could see directly into Meg's soul. "So, tell me about yourself. How have you been?"

Something about Mrs. Shay's motherly compassion made Meg want to unburden herself. "That's why I'm here," she said. "I had an accident and lost my memory. I need to know...I need to know everything about my past."

"Oh, my dear, I'm so sorry." Mrs. Shay pulled her chair closer to her desk and steepled her fingers. "Of course, I'll help in any way I can. Wait here while I get your files. I'll just be a few moments."

Meg held out her hand. "No. Not yet. I didn't realize you were here when I was, that you knew me then. I'd rather see myself through your eyes before reading about my past in a folder. Tell me what you remember."

Mrs. Shay smiled. "Of course. What do I remember about you? Well, the first time you came here, you were quiet, a little shy. You made friends with another girl right away. Her name was..."

"Lucy."

"Yes. Lucy. The two of you were inseparable. You did everything together."

Meg smiled. Somehow, she knew those were happy memories that held no danger to her. She hung on Mrs. Shay's every word, trying to recreate the memory of a little girl long forgotten.

Mrs. Shay chuckled. "You'd spend hours playing dominoes. I'd find them in the oddest places." She shook her head. "I tried to be firm with the two of you, but I just couldn't help letting you break a few rules. I was happy you had each other."

She let the rest go unspoken, but Meg could read between the lines. It must have been hard for a woman with so much love and compassion to see children suffer.

"You said the *first* time I came here."

Mrs. Shay nodded, her eyes darkening. "Your parents were...volatile. They had a history of drug use and criminal activity. But they wouldn't release you for adoption, and after a while they'd come back, claim they'd changed and take you home."

Meg didn't have to be a mind reader to see that Mrs. Shay disapproved. She wondered why. But this wasn't the time to push at long-buried secrets. Maybe there were some memories that should stay forgotten.

Mrs. Shay took a deep breath and let it out with a sigh. "They never kept you for long, though. Soon Social Services would bring you back to us. Each time you came back, you were a little more beaten down, a little sadder."

Meg's heart went out to that little unremembered girl. Mrs. Shay reached out and squeezed Meg's hand. There was something familiar about the tilt of her head, the compassion in her eyes.

Mrs. Shay glanced back at the pictures. "You were about the same age as my youngest daughter," she said. "It broke my heart to see you sad."

"I remember you," Meg said.

"You do? That's wonderful!"

"No. I mean, I remember your face from the pictures." Why hadn't she realized it sooner? "You used to wear your hair down. You're in all the pictures with us."

"Oh, yes. I was a counselor back then."

Meg frowned. "You had a pin on your collar. A dragonfly pin." Meg wasn't sure how to ask the question that weighed on her mind.

"You loved that pin," Mrs. Shay fingered her collar as if remembering the feel of it there. "You would stare at it while I was trying to counsel you, your thoughts far away. I'd tell you stories about the dragonfly to get you to focus on what I was saying—stories about transformation and change and protection. How the dragonfly is said to lead you through the mists of change to the wisdom of your soul."

Meg remembered Gemma's comment that the dragonfly warns us to be on the lookout for illusions and deceits. No wonder she felt it calling to her.

"You were obsessed with the dragonfly," Mrs. Shay continued. "With the pin at first, but then with the symbolism."

Meg closed her eyes. It made sense that a lost little girl would hang onto something that represented change and growth. "I have it," she said, choking on the words. How could she have stolen from this kind, gentle woman.

"Of course, you do." Mrs. Shay tipped her head. "I gave it to you."

Meg couldn't hide her surprise. "You gave it to me?"

Mrs. Shay's gaze turned inward. "It was at a very

low point in your life. Your parents had left you behind for the very last time. I promised you that things would get better one day, but you didn't believe me. You needed something to hang onto," she said. "You needed something to remind you that life would get better, that you wouldn't always be at someone else's mercy. So, I gave you the pin, and you told me you'd love it forever."

A tear blurred Meg's vision. "I guess I did. I still have it."

"And things did get better," she said. "I was at your wedding. You were radiant. That sad little girl had grown up to be a beautiful woman. I was so proud of you that day."

"I wish I could remember." Meg's thoughts drifted. And then, as if her thoughts conjured it, a wispy memory surfaced...

Lucy adjusted the simple white veil and fluffed Meg's hair around it. "Are you sure you want to go through with this?"

"I'm sure." Meg twisted her head and glared at Lucy. "Are you trying to talk me out of marrying Ben?"

"No. It's just that you haven't known him that long. I mean, he seems like a nice guy and all, but...I don't know. I guess I'm feeling a little jealous that I'm losing my best friend to a boy."

"You're not losing me, silly. Best friends forever, remember?"

"When we're apart and when we're together, we'll always remain blood sisters forever."

Meg couldn't believe Lucy remembered, but deep down she was secretly thrilled that she had.

Lucy handed Meg her bridal bouquet. "Okay, let's

do this."

They stood, and Meg gave Lucy an impetuous hug. "I can't believe I'm getting married! Did I forget anything?"

Lucy ticked off items on her fingers. "Let's see. Something old, something new, something borrowed, something blue. Nope. Haven't forgotten a thing."

Was it fantasy or reality? Were her memories trying to break through, or was she simply the victim of an overactive imagination? Meg couldn't be sure.

She told Mrs. Shay everything she could remember since she'd woken up in the hospital. It felt good to unburden herself. It was almost as if she was talking about someone else.

She wasn't sure when Mrs. Shay had taken her hand, but it was comforting. "And so, you see," she said. "I don't know who to believe."

"I can't answer that for you," Mrs. Shay said. "But I do know one thing. Lucy would lay down her life for you...and you for her. The two of you were closer than best friends. Closer even than sisters." She turned Meg's hand over and traced a faint scar. "Blood sisters."

Meg studied the scar. Had she done that? Did Lucy have a matching scar? Blood sisters.

"If Lucy is lying to you," Mrs. Shay said. "Then there's a very good reason for it. You can trust Lucy with your life."

Meg knew, deep down inside, that what the director said was true. "Mrs. Shay..."

"Carly," she squeezed Meg's hand. "Call me Carly."

Tears stung Meg's eyes. "Carly. Do you know if I

hurt my sister?"

"No." Mrs. Shay shook her head. "But I don't think you did. What do you think, Meg? Do you think you could have hurt your sister?"

Meg couldn't imagine a reason why she would. *No,* a voice in her head replied. *You'd never hurt anyone, especially someone you love.* The voice was firm, sure. It was Gemma's voice. "Didn't I tell anyone what happened?"

"You were traumatized. You never spoke of that night to me or anyone." She shook her head. "But I never believed it. No matter what they said."

"They?"

Mrs. Shay shook her head, a frown creasing her forehead. "Your parents. When they left you here, they said it was to protect your younger sister. They said you were jealous and took her out in the woods. Left her to die."

Meg put a hand to her mouth and stifled a gasp. She closed her eyes as flashes came one after another. Dark woods. A full moon. The smell of pine and the skitter of leaves beneath their feet. Running. Running. A child's voice crying out. *Meggy. Meggy stop, you're hurting me.*

Meg let out a cry. She shook her head and the vision faded. Was it real or had she simply imagined it? She had to find out the truth. "I need to find her," Meg said. "I need to find my sister."

"Are you sure?"

"Yes."

Mrs. Shay nodded. "Let me get your file. I can give you the last known address we had for your family. It's a place to start."

Alone in the room, Meg studied the family photos, Mrs. Shay's words echoing in her ears. *They anchor my heart.*

That's what family did, Meg realized. They anchored your heart. Even more reason to find her sister.

When Mrs. Shay returned with the folder, Meg copied down the last known address they had for her parents. She studied the few papers inside. Her sister's name was June. She was five years younger than Meg.

According to the papers, Meg was ten years old the last time her parents left her at St. Ophelia's. That meant her sister was only five. Did June remember her? Was she old enough to remember what happened that day? Maybe she wouldn't even want to see Meg.

Meg tucked the paper into her bag and thanked Mrs. Shay for being so helpful. "Oh, there's one more thing I wanted to ask. Why are there no pictures of Gemma on the walls?"

Mrs. Shay raised an eyebrow. "Gemma?"

"Yes, my friend Gemma. She said she was here with me. But I don't see her picture anywhere."

"Gemma." This time Mrs. Shay's voice was low and gentle. "Gemma is…was." She shook her head. "How do I put this?" She let out a slow breath. "Gemma isn't real."

Meg laughed. "Of course, she's real. I've spoken to her. She's been at my house."

The look in Mrs. Shay's eyes was sympathetic. "Honey, Gemma is—has always been—a figment of your imagination."

"No." Meg held her hand up in a warding-off gesture, as if she could stop the words before they reached her ears. "That's not true."

"What's her name?" Mrs. Shay asked. "Her full name."

Meg frowned, trying to remember. "I'm not sure. I know it starts with an I, though."

"Of course, you do." Mrs. Shay picked up a pen from the desk and wrote on the back of Meg's folder. *G-E-M-M-A-I.*

She turned the folder around and handed Meg the pen. "Write it backwards," she said.

Meg wrote, the truth dawning with each stroke of the pen. *I-A-M-M-E-G.*

I. AM. MEG.

No. She shook her head. *It can't be.*

"Gemma was your imaginary friend from the time you were little. She was the one you cried to at night, the one you whispered your secrets to."

Meg couldn't even fathom the idea that her imagination could produce something that could walk and talk and interact the way Gemma had. Meg tried to remember if anyone else had been around at the same time. Gemma just showed up when she needed her. "Not real?"

"She was real to you. She gave you comfort. She gave you strength." Mrs. Shay squeezed Meg's shoulder. "I think Gemma is the voice of your inner self, the voice of truth."

Meg was only half listening. She stared at the folder, the words burning into her brain.

I AM MEG.

Chapter Twenty-Six

Lucy coughed and waved the smoke away with a dish towel. She glared at the charred cupcakes as if they were to blame. She wasn't cut out for this cooking stuff. That was Meg's job. Meg was the one who worked magic in the kitchen. Lucy was the bookkeeper, the business brains.

But at this rate they wouldn't have a business. There was no money coming in, and they were losing some of their best clients who didn't have time to wait for Meg to lift herself out of this fog.

The smoke detector went off, and the doorbell rang at the exact same moment. Lucy glanced from one to the other and went to answer the door first. Meg standing in the doorway surprised her.

Meg glanced down at the tray of burnt cupcakes and wrinkled her nose. "No thanks."

"Sure, kick a girl when she's down."

Meg smiled and stepped inside. "The apron is a nice touch." It was white, frilly, and covered with pastel-colored dancing cupcakes. "The smoke detector, not so much, though."

"Glad you like it. It's yours." Lucy shouted and turned, then she dumped the entire batch of ruined cupcakes into the garbage. She climbed on a stepstool and pushed a button, silencing the smoke detector. "I hate to admit it, but this is my third try."

"Guess that means I'm not out of a job, huh?"

Lucy froze, holding her breath. She stepped down carefully and turned. "Does that mean you want to start working the cupcake truck again?"

Meg shrugged. "If you want."

Lucy took a deep breath. "No." She took Meg's hand and led her to the dining room table. "I mean yes, but…we can't be true partners until there's complete trust between us. I still haven't been totally honest with you."

"I know."

Lucy was taken aback. "You know?"

"Clay told me about St. Ophelia's. I went there, today, and Mrs. Shay told me everything."

Lucy felt a well of relief tighten her throat. "Thank God. I hated lying to you, Meg. I told Ben it wasn't right, but he thought we were protecting you."

"Protecting me from what?"

Lucy didn't think it was her place to say, but now that the truth was out, she owed it to her friend to be completely honest. "Ben didn't think your accident was…*an accident.*"

Meg tipped her head questioningly.

"He was convinced you'd tried to commit suicide."

"Suicide? Why in the world would I do that?"

Lucy stood and put a kettle on to boil. She took two cups from the cabinet and dropped teabags inside them before answering. "You were depressed. It got worse over the years. When the police told Ben there were no skid marks on the road, they implied…"

"That I drove the car into the tree on purpose?"

Lucy nodded.

Meg frowned, a thoughtful expression on her face.

"I don't know," she said. "It doesn't feel like something I'd do."

"I didn't think so either. But Ben was so afraid of losing you." She put a hand over her mouth and shook her head. "He was willing to do anything to save you from yourself."

Meg's voice was cold. "Including hiring people to pretend to be family members?"

Lucy shook her head. "I had nothing to do with that." But still she felt guilty for letting the charade go on as long as it had. "I should have put a stop to it," she admitted. I'm sorry, Meg."

Over tea, Lucy shared her memories with Meg, things only the two of them would know. It felt freeing. The worst part of Meg's amnesia was that Lucy had lost the parts of herself that lived in Meg's memory. But she could rebuild those memories. They could rebuild them together.

"One of the things I admired most about you," she told Meg, "is that you were a survivor. No matter how many times you were knocked down, you got back up again." Lucy frowned. "I think by taking away your past and all you'd fought to overcome. Ben was leaving you as defenseless as a baby. He may have had the best of intentions, but it backfired on all of us."

"Ben told me about the argument the two of you had," Lucy continued. "How upset you were about the cradle. Of course he had no idea why you reacted the way you did, and I didn't tell him what I knew about your past. So maybe there was a hint of doubt in my own mind. Even so," Lucy said, "I still couldn't believe you'd tried to commit suicide. That's not the Meg I knew."

Meg nodded. "If you knew me so well, then you knew Gemma too, right?"

Lucy blew out a breath. She would have loved to brush this question under the rug, but she could feel that the trust she'd fought so hard to repair was fragile. If she was going to be honest with Meg, she had to be honest about everything, even if it was painful.

"Gemma." She shook her head. "One of the biggest fights we had growing up was over Gemma. I tried to tell you she was all in your imagination, but you insisted she was real. You said I was just jealous of her." Lucy shrugged. "Maybe I was. Sometimes Gemma seemed more important to you than I was."

The wall she'd felt between them over the last months disappeared. Lucy caught a glimpse of the old Meg in an unguarded moment. That glimpse was all she needed. She'd wait as long as it took to win Meg's trust back and rebuild the friendship that was damaged but not destroyed.

"Thank you for being honest with me," Meg said. "We told each other everything?"

"Pretty much, yeah."

"So then, I guess I told you what happened with my sister?"

Lucy shook her head. She wished she could ease Meg's mind, but that was the one thing Meg had never shared. "No. I'm sorry. All I know is that you'd wake up screaming in the middle of the night. Screaming for Buggy."

"Buggy?"

"Your sister. You called her June, June Bug, Buggy. Depending on your mood."

Meg smiled. "Buggy," she whispered with a

faraway look in her face. "God, I wish I could remember." She reached in her purse and pulled out a slip of paper. "I need to find her, Lucy. Mrs. Shay gave me their last address. Since you're better at the computer than I am, I was hoping you'd help me track her down."

"Of course, I will," Lucy said. Even as she said it, however, she remembered those days as if it was yesterday. Meg hadn't spoken for weeks. Her eyes had been haunted, and she'd woken up screaming from nightmares she wouldn't share with anyone, not even her best friend. "Are you sure you want to do this, Meg?"

Meg nodded. "More than anything. I need to find out the real truth about what happened and why my parents abandoned me."

"Then I'll help in any way I can. If it's at all possible, we'll find her."

****

Back at the hotel, Meg had a lot to think about. She stood in the center of the room, pressed in on all sides by the weight of silence. She felt more alone than she'd ever felt before.

She was still angry at Ben for lying, but that anger was tempered by the knowledge that he believed he was saving her life. Still, he'd gone too far. It was one thing to sugar-coat the truth, another to invent an entire family and revised history. He shouldn't have played with her emotions that way.

She hated to admit it, but she missed them all. Sierra, her pretend sister. Mabel and Norm, her pretend parents, and their pretend two-story Colonial in the suburbs.

A tear slid down her cheek. Damn it! She missed having a family and people who cared about her, even if they were only actors on a stage. Their story may have been fiction, but the grief over losing them was real.

You still have me.

It was Gemma's voice she heard. But she knew Gemma wasn't real. Gemma was her own voice of reason.

Meg walked toward the mirror and frowned at her reflection. The image of Gemma floated over her own features like a chiffon mask. She looked the way Meg imagined she might have looked if life hadn't gotten in the way. Gemma was a part of herself. A wiser, more patient and understanding part of herself. The undamaged part.

"What do I do now?" Meg asked in a hushed whisper.

You do what we've always done. You stand up tall and stride forward, one foot in front of the other. We're survivors. If you can't remember that, then I'll remember for you.

Gemma's voice was her own. Had it always been that way? Why hadn't she noticed before?

A survivor. It held a ring of truth. Then the image she'd begun to form of poor, suicidal Meg didn't make sense. That Meg was a victim, tossed by fate and set adrift in a world she couldn't understand. Even Ben, who should know her better than anyone else, saw her as weak and vulnerable. His entire lie was based on the fact that he thought she'd tried to kill herself.

"I wouldn't," she said to her reflection. Then louder and with more commitment. "I would never try to kill myself. I don't give up. I may not remember much, but I know Lucy is right about one thing. I'm a survivor."

She picked up a piece of hotel stationary and began writing:

Dear Gemma:

I know you're not real, but I need your strength right now. I need your wisdom to guide me.

If you're a part of me, then you're the strongest part, the wisest part, the part that knows what has to be done and has the determination to do it.

No wonder you were the one I turned to in my darkest hours. I knew you'd carry my secrets to the grave with us. I knew you would never abandon me the way everyone else did.

You may not be real, Gemma, but you're the realest part of me.

Love,

Meg

Meg put down the pen. That night she slept peacefully for the first time since waking up in the hospital bed. There were no dreams, no tears, and no thrashing to escape from unremembered nightmares.

Chapter Twenty-Seven

Lucy called early the next morning. "I found her," she said, her voice brimming with excitement. "Her name is June Ellen Ford, and she lives about twenty minutes outside of town."

"June," Meg murmured. "June bug."

Lucy didn't seem to hear. "Listen," she said. "Why don't I pick you up in oh, about twenty minutes? We'll drive out there and you two can have a private chat. I'll stay in the car. Hopefully it will go well. If not, I'll be there waiting."

"Thank you for the offer, but it's okay. Really. You've done enough already."

"Hey, that's what friends are for." Her voice softened. "You may not remember what happened, but I remember how hurt you were. I think this is important, Meg. Even if she rejects you, it's important that you try."

"Okay. But I don't want to just barge in on her. I should call first and let her know I'm coming."

Lucy agreed and gave Meg the phone number she'd found, along with an address. "Give her a call," Lucy said. "Either way, I'm coming to get you. If your sister doesn't want to meet you, then we'll go out to breakfast and plan our next move."

It took Meg another ten minutes of staring at the number to finally work up the nerve to make the call.

The voice at the other end sounded young and jaded. "Is this June Ellen Ford?"

"Yes. Who's this?"

"My name is Meg. Meg Tyler. I think, um. I think I'm your sister."

A soft snort sounded at the other end of the line. "You must have the wrong number. I don't have a sister."

Of all the scenarios Meg had imagined, this wasn't one of them. "They never mentioned me at all?" It was bad enough her parents had turned their back on her, but they'd erased her from her sister's memories as well—as if she'd never existed.

Her voice hitched but she stumbled on. "They left me in a home for girls when I was about ten. You would have been four or five. Surely you remember something."

"Do you remember anything from when you were four?" June asked, her voice dripping with sarcasm.

Meg started to reply, then felt a bubble of hysteria rise in her chest. She tried to hold it back, but it escaped in a squeak, then burst from her lips in a laugh that began in her chest and rose until tears filled her eyes and the laughter turned to sobs—deep, heartbreaking sobs that tore away the weak veneer of control she'd been holding onto for so long. "No, I don't remember. I don't remember anything."

She filled June in on everything that had happened—from her accident, to losing her memory, to Ben's lies, then finding out she had a sister. "I may not remember you," she said, "but I know you're my sister, even if our parents never told you about me."

June's voice was gentle now. "You say they left

you behind?"

"Yes. They moved away and never came back."

June laughed again, a sound that held no humor. "Guess you were the lucky one. You got away."

Meg heard a baby's cry in the background. June had kids? That would make Meg an aunt. The thought filled her with pride and a new determination. "Can I come see you? Can we talk?"

There was a slight hesitation and Meg held her breath.

"Sure. I guess."

Meg exhaled with relief. "Thank you. Thank you. I'll be there in about an hour."

Meg didn't have to decide what to wear. She only had one clean outfit left—a heather-gray tunic and black leggings. She should have packed more but wasn't thinking. She'd just tossed a few things into an overnight bag and left. She'd have to go by the house and get some more clothes if she was going to stay away any longer. But not today. Today she had more important things to focus on.

Lucy arrived right on time. She glanced around the hotel room disapprovingly but didn't say anything. Meg had a feeling Lucy would have spoken her mind in the past, but their new relationship was still on fragile ground.

"Did you talk to her?" she asked.

"Yes." Meg grabbed her purse and followed Lucy out to the car. "She doesn't remember having a sister. My parents—our parents—never told her about me."

Lucy froze, one hand on the door handle. "Nothing?"

Meg shook her head. "Once they sent me away, I

ceased to exist. For them. For my sister. Gone. Like yesterday's trash." She took a deep breath. It made her so angry that they'd just tried to erase her out of existence. No wonder she made up imaginary friends.

Lucy held her gaze for a long moment, then broke the silence with a brusque, "They didn't deserve you."

Those four words brought Meg comfort. Not so much because it was true, but because that was exactly what a best friend would say.

Twenty minutes later they parked in front of a run-down apartment building. Meg took a deep breath, trying to work up her nerve.

"Are you sure you don't want me to go in with you?"

Meg shook her head. "No. She may be more likely to open up if it's just the two of us."

Lucy reached over and squeezed Meg's hand. "Okay. I'll be right here if you need me."

Meg nodded, then opened the car door. She stood on the sidewalk for a moment looking around. The apartment building looked tired, with paint peeling in curling strips and concrete steps pitted and chipped. She heard a child's voice and peeked over the fence to see a little girl on a swing in the side yard.

What might have been a memory floated to the surface. Meg saw another little girl's face superimposed over the child's. A sense of love, longing, and remembrance made her knees weak, then it was gone, leaving only the faintest shadow of the past behind as the present once again superimposed itself over the scene. The little girl on the swing looked up and smiled.

With a new determination, Meg marched to the front door and rang the bell. The woman who answered was tiny with hair the color of autumn wheat. She didn't look anything like Meg. As a matter of fact, Meg realized that Sierra looked more like her sister than this petite woman in the doorway.

Her eyes were clear and held a hint of humor. "I don't remember you."

"I don't remember you, either," Meg said. "But I don't remember anyone, so…"

June gestured toward the living room. "Come on inside. Can I get you coffee? Tea?"

"I'll have whatever you're having," Meg said.

"Tea for me." June glanced toward a baby's cradle across the room. "Breastfeeding," she explained.

She glanced back at Meg. "You look like her."

Meg blinked. She knew who June was talking about, but she didn't want to think about the mother who'd abandoned her. Today was about reconnecting with her sister. There'd be time to answer other questions down the road.

While June prepared the tea, Meg looked around. The apartment was shabby but clean. Toys and children's books lay in cluttered piles. A framed photograph showed three children in a posed studio shot.

June came back holding a tray with two cups of tea and a plate of cookies. "I don't usually keep cookies in the house," she said. "But the girl next door was selling them for Girl Scouts, so I splurged."

Meg smiled. She pointed to the picture she'd spotted earlier. "You have three kids?"

June nodded. "Harley is four and a half. It's important to remember the half, or she'll be terribly offended. She's outside right now. Tommy just turned three but still has a tight grip on the Terrible Twos. He's having a play date with the little boy next door. I'll treat his mother to wine and cheese tonight and return the favor next week." She glanced at the cradle across the room. "That little peanut is six months old. His name is Jeremy, but we call him Sprout. He's the happiest baby I've ever seen."

Meg blurted out, "But you're only…"

"Twenty-three. Right." She shrugged. "Guess I'm an overachiever."

"I didn't mean…"

But the baby started fussing, and June got up and walked to the cradle, leaving the sentence hanging unfinished. She scooped the baby up on her shoulder where he gurgled and cooed. June's face glowed with love, and again Meg felt a sense of loss coupled with heartbreaking rage. Her arms ached to hold the baby. "May I?" she asked.

June gently handed the baby to Meg, and he snuggled warm and sweet against her neck. Meg felt some of the anger drain from her body. This child was her nephew. The thought was like a balm to her wounded past.

Family. They anchor you.

"You're a natural," June said. "Do you have kids?"

Meg shook her head. "No. Not yet." She took a deep breath, inhaling the intoxicating scent of baby. He curled his little fist around her finger, and her heart swelled with yearning.

June smiled. "This is what life's all about," she said, her gaze locked on the baby. "Loving someone who loves you back."

"Your life wasn't easy, was it?

June shrugged. "You escaped when you were ten years old. It took me twenty years to escape. Then I jumped from one abuser to another. Seems to be a pattern."

Meg nodded. A pattern. Maybe that explained her intoxication with Clay. "Tell me about your husband."

June looked away, gazing into the distance. "I married an abuser," she said, confirming Meg's suspicions. June shook her head. "But I broke the cycle and left him. I don't want my kids to have to go through what I did. They're better off with no father at all than an abusive one." She held Meg's gaze. "You should know that."

"There are a lot of things I *should* know," Meg admitted. "But the truth is, the more I discover, the less I *want* to know about my past."

"You know what the most important thing about the past is?"

"What's that?"

"The most important thing about the past is that it's *in the past*. You can't change it. You can only change the way you react to it."

Meg stared at June, who seemed far wiser than her twenty-three years. "When I lost my memory, my husband tried to shield me from my past," she said. "I'd been in a coma for weeks. He thought I tried to kill myself."

"Did you?"

"I don't think so. No, that just doesn't feel right. But Ben didn't know that, and he thought he could save me by writing a new history of my past that was all sweetness and light."

"Well, in my opinion, you don't need Ben or

anyone else to do that for you. You can do it yourself. You can be bitter or choose not to be."

"I suppose." Meg shook her head. "I understand why he did it, but I can't forgive Ben for lying to me about everything. I walked away."

June lifted her sleeve and Meg was horrified to see scars and old burn marks. "This is abuse," she said. "This is something you stand up and walk away from."

June lowered her sleeve again, hiding the scars, but Meg couldn't help wondering what other scars were hidden beneath her clothes. "I'm sorry," she said.

June shrugged. "Your husband told a lie. He started with a little white lie to protect you. That doesn't seem so terrible in the scheme of things now, does it?"

Meg was ashamed of herself. In light of the abuse her sister had obviously undergone before putting an end to her relationship, a lie didn't seem worth throwing a marriage away over—especially a lie told with the best of intentions. Running away wasn't the answer, either.

Just then, the little girl from the swing came running inside. "Mommy, Mommy." She stopped when she spotted Meg.

She looked so familiar, with her lopsided ponytail, the same wheat colored hair as June, and a smattering of freckles across her cheeks.

Buggy.

June reached forward and wiped a smudge of dirt from the girl's cheek with her thumb. "This is Harley," she said. "Her father had a thing for motorcycles."

Meg leaned forward. Before she could stop herself, the words flew out of her mouth. "How are you, Buggy?"

The little girl crinkled her nose. But it was June who stared at her strangely. "Where did you hear that name? Buggy?"

"It just came out."

June took a deep breath. "My father called me June Bug. But someone...I remember someone calling me Buggy." She looked at Meg with tears misting her eyes. "I think it was you."

"I'm not Buggy," the little girl said, her lips curled into a pout.

"I'm sorry," Meg said. "I got confused. You're Harley, right?"

The girl nodded, still not sure whether to forgive Meg for her transgression, although Meg suspected it wasn't as terrible as leaving the half year off her age would have been.

"This is Meg," June told her daughter. She glanced at Meg with a knowing smile. "She's your Aunt Meg."

Harley's eyes widened. "My aunt? I've always wanted an aunt!"

"And I've always wanted a niece," Meg said, tears clouding her vision. Even without a memory, Meg knew she was speaking the truth.

Harley came closer and with the innocence of youth, asked, "Where have you been all my life?"

"I was lost," Meg said. And that too was the truth.

"I think you're right," she said to June. "Why obsess over an unremembered life when I should be busy building a new one?"

"Exactly. "It's a perfect opportunity to reinvent who you are. Like a *Get Out of Jail Free* card."

Meg thought about her beautiful home and the life she had with Ben. It wasn't jail by a long shot. It was embarrassing to think about how much she'd taken for granted when her sister had so little.

But all that was going to change now that she had June and her children back in her life.

Chapter Twenty-Eight

Meg had Lucy drive her back to the hotel just long enough to pick up her few belongings and check out of the room.

Lucy was delighted to hear that Meg was going to move back home and try to work things out with Ben. "Maybe we could get the cupcake truck rolling again?"

"Yeah, I think that's a great idea. But leave the baking to me, okay?"

"Not a problem," Lucy said.

To be honest, Meg was looking forward to feeling useful again. She'd been excited by the cookbooks she'd found in the kitchen, and she itched to try some of the cupcake recipes. Lucy told her she had more recipes saved on the computer and promised to show Meg where to find them.

Lucy dropped Meg off at her house. "Are you sure you don't want me to drive you anywhere else?"

"No," she said. "I think I'm going to walk over to the campus and surprise Ben. It's a beautiful day, and I could use the fresh air."

After Lucy left, Meg put her overnight bag in the guest room. Although willing to give her marriage another try, she wasn't quite ready to share their marital bed. She hoped the day would come, but until she truly felt she could trust Ben again, she'd stay in the guest room.

Despite everything, Meg felt a weight lifted from her shoulders as she walked the short distance to the campus. The sun seemed brighter, the grass greener and her step lighter. Although Meg still didn't know exactly what had happened with her sister the day she was left behind for good at St. Ophelia's, she was ready to put the painful past behind her and start fresh. It took a few moments before she realized someone was calling her name.

She turned and saw Sierra rushing toward her. Meg held up her hand. "I don't want to talk to you. I know you're not my sister.

Sierra at least had the decency to look ashamed. "I know. Ben told me."

"I know you lied. But why?" Meg shook her head. "What would possess you to take part in such a farce?"

"I don't know. At first, I did it to please Ben. Then it became a challenge, like the greatest acting job in the world. And then..." her voice trailed off. "Then I started to enjoy being your little sister. I lost myself in the role." She looked down and shuffled her feet. I know I'm not your real sister. But our experiences were real, the talks we had were real, and the emotions we shared were real."

"No. They were all based on a lie. I don't need you in my life." Even when she said it, however, Meg knew it wasn't all true. She still had feelings for Sierra—maybe not as a sister, but as a new friend. And if she could forgive Ben, she certainly could forgive Sierra for going along with him.

"I never set out to hurt you, Meg. I didn't even know you. I just thought it was a way for me to get closer to Ben."

At Meg's shocked expression, Sierra waved her hands. "Not like that. I mean, he's so talented. I wanted some of that magic to rub off on me. I wanted to absorb his writing secrets so I could be the same kind of writer he is."

Seeing Ben through someone else's eyes—even if it was a star-struck student—made her see him in a new light.

"Have you read his book?" Sierra asked.

Meg shook her head. "I'm sure I read it before the accident, but not since."

"You should. It's wonderful. And he's writing again. He's writing your story. The fact that he wrote this entire story for you only proves what a great writer he is. Maybe he can publish it and call it *Meg's Story*."

"Or *Not Her Story*," Meg said. They both laughed, and it was refreshing to let the anger go. "I don't even know what my real story is," Meg admitted.

"Oh, but *I* do, Meg. I know you better than you know yourself." She reached in her tote bag, pulled out a tattered notebook and handed it to Meg. "I read your journal."

Meg gasped and reached for the book. "You read my journal? My private journal?"

Sierra lowered her eyes. "I justified it by telling myself I was researching a part. I needed to be believable, but…"

"But what?" Meg demanded.

"But the truth is, I thought you didn't deserve Ben. I guess, I was hoping to prove it to him."

Meg was almost afraid to ask. "What did you discover."

Sierra looked up with tears in her eyes. "I know

your secrets, your sorrows, how deeply you love and how desperately you fear being abandoned. I can empathize with the person who wrote on these pages— the person you've forgotten. And I want to help you find her again if you'll let me."

Meg clutched the journal to her chest. She wanted to find that person as well.

****

Meg changed her mind about going to see Ben on campus. She'd talk to him when he came home from class. For now, she had more important things to do.

With the journal clutched to her chest, she turned and walked the few short blocks to her favorite bench at the park. There she sat, prepared to read the most important book in the world—her own story told in her own words.

Dear Gemma,

It's a new year and a new journal. How long have I been writing to you? Maybe fifteen years now? It started when I was young. I guess ten or so. About the time I knew I'd never be leaving St. Ophelia's.

It seems easier, somehow, pretending to write to someone who doesn't exist. But you've always been there for me when I needed you most, so why stop now?

I've been toying with the idea of turning these journals into a book for other women who need to find their true selves. Kind of a quasi-memoir of sorts. The only thing stopping me is wondering how it would affect Ben. He's been so paralyzed by fear that he can't write a word. Fear of what? Fear of failure or fear of success?

I don't know. It's probably a silly idea anyway.

Stronger,

I AM MEG

Meg smiled. The words sounded like her, but different as well. She continued reading. The journal was filled with random thoughts, snippets of poetry and more letters to Gemma—stories about her life, about her dreams, about healing and letting go of the past.

No wonder it had felt so natural to write a note to Gemma in the hotel room. It was something she'd been doing all of her life, pouring her heart out to an imaginary friend and confidante. On the pages, she discovered a woman who was damaged but not bitter. A woman who was resilient and strong.

Reading the bits of verse sprinkled among the pages, Meg saw an innocence there. This was not the voice of someone struggling with depression or contemplating suicide.

I'll sit on a swing in the meadow
My lacy scarf caught on a breeze
My gaze will be yearning and pensive
My hand lightly draped on my knee
If I were a cover-girl model
How pretty and stately I'd be

"Nope, not suicidal at all."

Meg recognized the voice. She wasn't surprised to see Gemma sitting on the bench beside her, pointing to the poem in the journal."

"I know you're not real."

Gemma shrugs. "What's real, anyway? You're real, and I'm a part of you, so that makes me real."

A tear slid down Meg's cheek. "I think writing to you saved my life, Gemma."

"I think *you* saved your life."

Meg blinked away the tears. There was one more

thing she had to do. She turned to the very last page to see what she'd written before the accident.

Dear Gemma,

I've come to a decision. I know now why the thought of getting pregnant filled me with such fear. Between the trauma of seeing my pregnant mother bleeding on the floor after another beating at my father's hands, the heartbreak of losing Clay's baby, and my fear that Ben would leave me too once he found out I was pregnant, it's no wonder the thought scared me to death.

But I've worked that all out on these pages and honestly, I'm tired of lying to Ben. He wants a baby so desperately. It would rip his heart out if he knew I'd been taking birth control pills all these months. But I'm ready now. I'm ready to start a family. I'll tell Ben tonight. But first I'm going to the grocery store to pick out some things for a nice romantic dinner. Then I'll tell Ben everything and hope he forgives me. Maybe tonight we'll start the family we both want.

Determined,

I AM MEG

Wow. So Ben wasn't the only one who'd lied. Meg was ashamed to see that she was guilty as well. But there was still time to make things right.

She looked up, but Gemma was gone. Just then a dragonfly landed on the pages of her journal. It stayed there a moment, translucent wings shimmering on the page. Somehow Meg knew it was a sign that she was making the right decision.

****

The moment Ben came in the door and spotted Meg, his face brightened, and he looked as though a weight had been lifted from his shoulders. He rushed toward her, "Meg, I'm so glad you're home. I've been worried sick." He stepped back and held her gaze. "You are coming home, right?"

Meg nodded. "But there are things we have to discuss."

"Yes." He blew out a breath. "Meg, I can't tell you how sorry I am. I swear I thought I was doing the right thing, but then it got out of control, and I couldn't seem to stop."

"I know," Meg said. "And I'd be a hypocrite to keep blaming you for what you did, when I lied myself. If we're going to make this work, we have to promise never to lie to each other again—for any reason. No more secrets, no more lies."

"Yes," Ben said. "But..." His eyes widened when he noticed the journal on the counter. His jaw dropped. "Where did you find that?"

"My journal?

"Yes. I found it tucked between the cushions of the couch when you were in the hospital. I was afraid that reading it would send you back into whatever depressed state you were in when you crashed the car, so I hid it in my desk at work. How did you find it?"

"Sierra gave it to me."

Ben shook his head, a puzzled look on his face. "How did she get it?"

"I thought you..."

"No," he exclaimed. "That was private. I'd never let someone else read it. Even I didn't want to read it at first, but then, I thought maybe there was something inside that would help you get your memory back. But once I started reading it, I was afraid the memories were too painful for you. I couldn't continue and put it in my desk for safekeeping." Ben wiped his brow. "Oh God, I've done everything wrong, haven't I?"

Meg smiled. "No. But one thing should ease your mind. Maybe I was depressed, and maybe I wasn't thinking clearly. But there's no way I tried to commit suicide. Lucy said I'm a survivor, and this journal proves that. Maybe if you'd read it all the way through, you wouldn't have felt compelled to write an entirely new history for me."

"I'm sorry. I'm sorry for making a mess of things."

"You're not the only one," she admitted. "I read in my journal that I'd miscarried Clay's baby when I was a teenager. I called Lucy who confirmed it, and she said I'd made her promise never to tell anyone, especially you."

He reached out to take her hand. "Oh honey, I'm so sorry. If I'd known, maybe I'd have been more understanding. Maybe I wouldn't have pushed so hard to have a baby."

Meg nodded, tears welling in her eyes. "I'm learning that buried secrets can be even more harmful than lies." She shook her head. "I want a fresh start, Ben. No more secrets and no more lies."

Ben squeezed her hand. "I want that as well, Meg. A fresh start with the woman I married, not the one I created."

"Even if I'm not perfect?"

Ben gave her a crooked grin. "Perfection is boring. Even fictional characters need a few flaws to make them believable."

"Speaking of fiction, I'd like to read your book. If that's all right."

"All right? Are you kidding me?"

Without waiting for a response, he jumped up and rushed to his desk, grabbed a copy and handed it to her. He leaned over her shoulder and opened the book to the dedication page.

With fresh tears blurring her vision, Meg read:

For Meg, my light, my love, my inspiration.

Chapter Twenty-Nine

As the months went by, Meg and Ben settled into a comfortable life together. It was a good life, made up of slow, easy sunsets rather than skies ablaze with fireworks. Ben was strong, dependable, and kind— every woman's dream of a husband. But there was a wall of lost memories keeping them apart. And because they'd promised no more lies, she'd told Ben about her one night with Clay. The ghost of her infidelity haunted their marriage.

It was the same with Lucy. They worked together, laughed together, made new memories together. But they could never be as close as they once were when only one of them remembered their shared past.

Meg and Ben had separate bedrooms, separate routines. They were more like roommates than husband and wife. Part of her was playing a role and the other part sat back observing and searching for clues.

She and Lucy had gone back to work, and she was happy to say, the cupcake business was booming.

She had a new, but blossoming, relationship with her sister June, and delighted in being called Auntie Meg by June's children, savoring sweet, sticky hugs and toothless smiles.

And Gemma was still the voice of wisdom in her head. She knew Gemma was a part of herself, a part she could rely on to have her best interests at heart. They had long conversations in the still of the night. And she continued to use Gemma as a device in her journals. It felt comfortable. Just writing "Dear Gemma" seemed to open up the floodgates, allowing Meg to express her deepest secrets and fears and hopes for the future.

The days went by and she smiled, but the smile was a mask and there was a bitter seed of distrust buried deep in her heart that she couldn't shake. Most of the time she felt hollow, an observer to her life rather than a participant. Had she always felt that way? No, not according to the pages in her journal.

Sometimes she'd catch Ben when he didn't know she was looking and see a sadness in his eyes, a yearning for something that no longer existed. She wished she could fix that, but it was beyond her ability to repair.

Meg had adapted to a life without memories. Memories only kept people anchored to an unforgiving past. Better to live in the now, to embrace the future. Yes, she was content. Maybe even happy. At least, she thought so. And then everything changed.

Dear Gemma,

I missed my period last month. Today my pregnancy test was positive. That should be a good thing, right? Except Ben and I haven't made love since that night after we went to dinner at Milano's Restaurant. And then there was that one night of reckless passion with Clay.

So, the question is, whose baby am I carrying?

Confused,

I AM MEG

The first person Meg told was June. If anyone would understand, it would be her sister.

Her *real* sister.

They'd grown closer over the past few months, and the children were accustomed to Meg showing up with bags full of toys and groceries. It had taken some time to convince June to accept what she considered charity, but since Meg focused primarily on things the kids needed, June graciously accepted the nutritious snacks and warm clothes. After all, Meg had fallen immediately and completely in love with her niece and nephews.

Harley spotted her as soon as she arrived and threw the door open. "Auntie Meg," she cried. Hearing her name, Tommy toddled in and the two of them threw themselves at her, chattering for her attention. Meg set the cake box on the coffee table, then lifted Tommy into her arms and took Harley's hand.

"Hey, Buggy," she said entering the kitchen. It was a name that fell naturally from her lips, and one that June enjoyed. It was something special between just the two of them.

June spotted the bakery box. "Is that cake?"

"Yep. I thought we might celebrate today."

"Great timing." June held up a piece of paper. "I got my GED today."

June had been preparing for the high-school equivalency exam for months now, and Meg couldn't be more proud. She gave June a big hug, and then settled down with Tommy on her lap. "Congratulations. You've worked hard and deserve to celebrate. I'm glad I picked up a cake. "

June put the kettle on to boil. Tea had become a regular part of their routine, and they'd often spend an afternoon sampling gourmet tea at a local shop. "How does Moroccan Mint sound today?"

"That'll go perfect with the chocolate cake." Meg bounced Tommy on her knee and listened to the adventures of Harlan's day at pre-school while June prepared the tea and cut slices of cake.

Once they'd eaten their cake, the kids ran off to play, leaving Meg and June alone to talk. Meg smiled at the children as they dumped out the dominoes she'd bought them last week and began building a chain to topple over…just like she'd taught them.

"So, what's the occasion?" June asked, clearing the dishes from the table.

"Well." Meg couldn't stop the smile from breaking out on her face. "You know how much I love being an aunt to your kids, right?"

"Sure."

Meg caught herself grinning. "I thought maybe *you'd* like to know how much fun it is to be an aunt."

June jumped up, nearly knocking over her teacup. "Seriously? You're pregnant?"

"I am," Meg said, overwhelmed with a jumble of emotions. She was happy, but… She cleared her throat. "There is one little problem."

June gave her a questioning look, then understanding washed over her features. "Oh."

Meg had told June everything about those first few weeks out of the hospital, including her infatuation and indiscretion with Clay.

"Didn't you say you'd read in your journal that you'd lost Clay's baby once before?"

Meg nodded. She'd talked to Lucy about it, but Lucy had just said it was a bad time in her life, and she shouldn't think about it. Better to focus on the future than dwell on the past. Which was true, but...

"I'm going to have to talk to Ben. I promised him no more secrets or lies between us." A frown crossed her brow. "And then there's Clay. He's not good for me, and he wouldn't be a good father. I'm afraid he'd be the same type of man you and I both escaped from."

June reached across the table and squeezed Meg's hand. "It's okay. Whatever you discover, remember you can break the cycle. I did. The past doesn't define us, and we don't have to settle for someone abusive in our life, whether he's the biological father of our children or not."

Meg knew that June was speaking from experience. Even if the baby belonged to Clay, that didn't mean he had to be a part of Meg's life. "I know that Ben would love and care for the child, no matter what. But is that fair to him?"

June shrugged. "It's not the moment of planting a seed that makes a man a father. It's the days and months and years that come afterward, shaping a life, being there for the first everything—first tooth, first steps, first day of school."

As if on cue, the baby started fussing. June went to the cradle and lifted him up, then brought him to Meg. He was warm and sleepy in her arms and curled up against her neck with total trust. She inhaled the sweet baby scent, knowing she'd do anything in the world to protect him and keep him safe.

June smiled. "You love him, don't you?"

"With all my heart."

"Even though you're not his biological mother?"

"Yeah," Meg smiled. "Good point."

"Well, here's another good point, since I'm on a

roll." She held Meg's gaze, her face serious. "If neither man steps up to the plate, you can do this alone. You don't need anyone who isn't the right fit in your life and your child's life. It's your choice."

Meg held her nephew close, sure of one thing. She wanted to have this baby, with or without the baby's father...whoever he may be.

****

Meg stayed longer than she should have, not only because she enjoyed being with June and the kids, but also because she was putting off having the conversation with Ben. What if this was the final straw and he walked away? She'd read enough in her journal to understand her deep-rooted fear of abandonment. But knowing the root cause didn't ease the fear.

When Ben walked in the door, Meg was dressed in one of her nicest outfits and had put some make-up on and spritzed herself with Ben's favorite cologne.

"Wow, what's the occasion?" he asked.

Her smile trembled only a tiny bit. "I made reservations for us to go to that place we liked— Milano's Italian Restaurant."

"Really?"

The hopeful expression on his face was almost too much for Meg to bear. Maybe she shouldn't have chosen a restaurant that held so many good memories for them as a couple, but she thought it would be a good way to lead into the conversation they had to have.

"Let me just change real quick." He leaned forward and planted a kiss on her cheek.

Meg felt terrible for getting his hopes up only to dash them again when he heard what she had to say.

****

Ben was animated on the ride to the restaurant. She let him chatter, lost in her own thoughts. Inside they were led to a semi-private booth in the corner, just as she'd requested. Ben seemed surprised when she ordered ice water instead of her usual glass of wine, but other than a raised eyebrow, he let it go unnoticed.

In the months since Meg had found her journal, she'd discovered four more hidden away. They made fascinating reading, but it was as if she was reading about someone else's life, not her own. There were still mysteries to be uncovered, and unanswered questions, but her journey was one of determination and perseverance.

She thought of June raising her kids alone, studying for her GED, and working nights typing medical transcripts when the kids were tucked in bed. She too had an inner core of strength that hadn't been beaten out of her. Despite the fact that their lives had veered off in different directions, they were more alike than different.

"Penny for your thoughts," Ben said.

Meg swirled the water in her glass. "I was just thinking how much June and I are alike, even though we were raised differently."

"Despite everything, you both survived."

"Yes, but she had it harder than I did." Meg held Ben's gaze for a long moment. "I had you. That made a big difference. I don't want to think what my life would be like if I'd stayed with Clay all those years ago."

"You'd have survived. I truly believe that, Meg. No one or nothing would have kept you down for long." His voice was sincere, even though it must have pained him to bring Clay's name into the conversation.

"Lucy said I was a survivor above all else."

Ben nodded. "Lucy knows you better than anyone else."

"Longer, maybe. Not necessarily better."

Ben's smile was genuine. He nodded, as if acknowledging how hard it was for Meg to admit that.

"I know it upsets you to bring up Clay, but he's an important part of tonight's conversation." Meg held up her hand to keep Ben from interrupting. She had to get the words out before she lost her nerve. "Remember the last time we were here?"

"Yes, of course." He smiled. She could see he was reliving that evening as well, and what happened afterward.

"I'm pregnant, Ben."

His eyes widened and his face lit up like a little boy on Christmas morning. "Oh honey, that's fantastic news! You're happy too, right, Meg? Does this mean we can go back to being husband and wife? Like it used to be?"

Meg desperately hoped so. But she hadn't dropped the final bomb yet. "Maybe. Remember we said this marriage would only work if there were no more secrets or lies?"

"Of course."

Meg watched Ben's face fall as the realization sunk in. "Clay."

"Yes." She'd been totally honest with Ben and told him about her one-night stand with Clay. He'd forgiven her and they'd put it behind them, along with all the other hurts and misunderstandings. But now there was a baby to think about. A baby whose paternity was in question. Could their marriage survive this on top of everything else?

Ben reached out and took her hand. "It doesn't matter, Meg. Once we'd talked about adopting if we weren't able to have a baby of our own. I would have loved a baby we'd adopted, and I'll love this baby no matter what. I promise you that."

Meg knew he was telling the truth. Ben was a good man, and his heart was full of enough love for a houseful of children. "I know you will, Ben. But I still have to tell Clay. We both know how badly things can go wrong when they're based on a lie. I don't want to start our baby's life that way."

Ben nodded. "*Our* baby. That's the key word, Meg." He gave her hand a squeeze. "You're right. Clay deserves to know. But either way, we're a team and we'll raise this baby together."

Chapter Thirty

There was one person who didn't agree with Meg's decision.

"No," Lucy said when Meg told her about the baby. "Clay doesn't deserve to know. He'll just use the information to worm his way back into your life."

They were loading cupcakes into the food truck. Meg wiped her hands on her apron. "He can't. I know better now. I won't fall for his charms."

Lucy gave her a doubtful look but didn't press the issue. She took the trays from Meg and loaded them into the special rack they'd built into the truck's cabinets. "I was there," she said. "You may not remember, but I do. I cried with you, brought you ice cream, and listened when you swore you'd never see him again."

She gave Meg a meaningful stare. "I was the one who found you bleeding at the bottom of the stairs when you lost his baby." Lucy slammed her fist on the countertop. "And the bastard never called, never came to see if you were all right. So no, I don't think he deserves anything."

Meg wrapped her arms around Lucy. She could feel the anger trembling through her friend's body. "It's okay, Luce. I'm not that damaged little girl anymore. I can stand up to Clay."

"Yeah," Lucy picked up a frosting knife and

brandished it through the air. "Guess you don't need me to protect you anymore, huh?"

"No," Meg said with a chuckle. "But I still need you to be my best friend."

"Best friends," Lucy said.

"Blood sisters forever," Meg finished. "Now unless you plan on frosting a cupcake, put down the knife and tell me where we're headed today."

"Okay, enough dramatics." Lucy sniffed and swiped her eyes. "Let's get this cupcake show on the road. First stop, Chucky's Diner. They've increased their order from two dozen to three. After that, we posted a few stops on Facebook—the parking lot at the mall, in the park, and in front of the college. If we're more than two minutes late at each stop, there will be an angry mob waiting for their cupcakes. After that, we're on our own. We'll just drive around and surprise people."

The day went quickly. By the time they were done, there were only two lonely cupcakes left on the rack. Meg closed the take-out window and handed one to Lucy. They sat back and toasted to another successful day with Sweet Sensations.

Lucy licked the frosting from her fingertips, then looked up at Meg. "So, when are you going to talk to Clay?"

"Tonight."

"You sure you don't want me there for moral support?"

Meg picked up the empty cupcake wrappers threw them in the garbage bin. "No. This is something I have to do myself."

"Okay. Just promise me you'll call if you need

me."

Meg promised, then added, "I'll always need you." And even without all of her memories, Meg knew that to be true.

****

Once she arrived at Clay's apartment, Meg wished she'd taken Lucy up on her offer. Her stomach clenched and every nerve in her body was on high alert. There was no reason to feel as if she was in danger, but for some unknown reason, she did.

He opened the door, a smug smile on his face. "I knew you'd come back."

When Clay leaned in for a kiss, she turned her head, avoiding his touch. "That's not why I came here."

He looked unconvinced. Meg was pretty sure he thought he could easily change her mind. Why not? Hadn't she fallen into his bed without a second thought? But that was then, this was now. "May I come in?"

"Of course." He stepped aside and gestured her inside. "Can I get you something to drink? Wine?"

"No thank you. I won't be here long. First, I want to thank you for telling me the truth about my past. I went to St. Ophelia's and confirmed everything you told me."

The self-satisfied smirk that crossed his face erased any trace of handsomeness, making Meg wonder what she'd seen in him besides his looks. He was all flash and no substance. Maybe it had been appealing to a teenage girl who didn't think she deserved better, but Meg knew what it felt like to be treated with respect— to be treated like an equal. The way Ben treated her. Why had it taken her so long to realize it?

"You didn't tell me everything though," she said, watching as conflicting emotions crossed his face.

He finally settled on taking the injured party tactic. "Look, if you're talking about that little mistake all those years ago, then it's okay. I forgive you. Water under the bridge."

"Little mistake? We're talking about a child."

He shrugged. "So you said. I think it was just a ploy to get me to marry you. But that's understandable. You were young and desperate to escape that orphanage, even if it meant lying about being pregnant."

Lying?

She kept her voice firm, not letting her emotions show. "There was a baby, Clay. I miscarried. And you *were* the father."

"How do I know that?" he said. "You could have been with anyone."

"I was sixteen," she cried. "Living in a home for girls. Where and when would I have the opportunity to be with anyone else?"

Clay let out an exasperated breath. "Like I said, water under the bridge."

She was tempted to leave without telling him she was pregnant. He didn't deserve to be a father. But she couldn't be a hypocrite and justify lying no matter what the reason. She had to tell him the truth, or she wouldn't be able to live with herself.

She spoke fast, anxious to get it over with. "No," she said. "It's not water under the bridge. Not when we're dealing with the same situation again."

It took a moment for understanding to hit him. "No, you're not…"

"I am."

Clay slammed his fist against the wall, causing Meg to flinch. "How the fuck did this happen? And how do I even know it's mine?"

His words were like a fist punching holes in her memory. One, two, three, it all came back, and she heard those exact same words coming from his mouth another day, another time.

"How do I even know the baby is mine?" His face was a mask of anger, his fists clenched, his eyes cold and hard.

"What? Clay, I was a virgin when we first made love."

"Well, that doesn't mean you stayed that way, does it?"

Meg was shocked. She couldn't believe the things he was saying to her, or the hatred in his eyes. "We're having a baby, Clay. What are we going to do?"

"We?" His voice rose in volume. "This is not my problem, sweetheart. You got yourself into this situation, you figure out how to deal with it." He turned to walk away.

She clutched his arm, desperate to make him stay, but he pushed her aside. When she wouldn't let go, he raised his fist and backhanded her. Hard. She remembers falling, falling, falling, and calling his name while holding a protective hand over her belly.

But he kept walking, leaving her bleeding at the base of the stairs. He walked away and never looked back.

The memory was as fresh as if it happened yesterday. "I lost the baby that day," she said. "And you didn't even care."

How could she have forgotten? He'd hit her, and she'd miscarried. He'd left her bleeding on the floor, and she'd sworn that day that no man would ever raise his hand to her again.

He'd gone to jail…not because of what he'd done to her, but over some stupid juvie offense. By the time he got out, she'd met Ben. Ben, who was safe, and honest, and true. Ben, who fixed her broken pieces and loved her for who she was. And she'd loved him too. Maybe not the way she'd girlishly lusted for Clay, but it was a mature love that grew and blossomed in solid soil.

The memory opened a floodgate. Cracks began to form, and more memories surfaced, then they all come tumbling down, like dominoes—clackity clack, clickety clack. One after another—her sister (click), her mother (click), Lucy, Clay, Ben (click, click, click). They were all there, all the lost days of her life.

But she didn't have the luxury of examining them just yet.

Clay was still trying to worm his way out of taking any responsibility. "Besides," he said, "it was only that one night, and I used a condom. So don't go trying to blame me for this."

He had, Meg realized. Why hadn't she remembered that he'd used a condom? It couldn't be his baby. The tightness in her chest loosened as relief washed over her. They'd still have to take a DNA test to rule him out for sure, but her instincts told her she'd worried for nothing. Clay had no claim on this child she was carrying. It was Ben's baby. Hers and Ben's.

Now that she remembered everything, Meg knew there was no way she'd have gone back and had an affair with Clay while she was married to Ben. He'd lied about that as well.

He was right about one thing, however. Their past was water under the bridge, and she could leave him behind once and for all without a single regret.

Chapter Thirty-One

Twenty-One Years Ago, Tinder Falls

Megan held her breath when she heard footsteps coming down the hallway. They were hard and heavy, her father's work boots rather than her mother's flippity floppities. She closed her eyes tight, pretending to be asleep, whispering her nightly prayer, "Please don't let him come in here, please don't let him come in."

The footsteps stopped outside her door. She tried not to make a sound and focused on counting her heartbeats instead. Fifteen heartbeats later, the steps moved on, and Megan let out a sigh of relief.

Until she realized the direction the footsteps were headed.

Megan slipped out of bed, tiptoed to the door, and opened it a crack. She saw her father entering her sister's bedroom and her heart gave a lurch.

No. June was only five. Only...only the same age Megan was when her father first started coming to her at night.

Megan ran down the hall and rushed into her sister's room. June was crouched in the corner, her blanket pulled up over her chest and her eyes wide. The fear on June's face told Megan this wasn't the first time.

Overcome with a nameless rage, Megan rushed

across the room and began pushing her father and pounding him with her fists. "Don't you touch her. Don't you dare touch her!"

Her father simply laughed. "Feisty, ain't you, little girl? So, what are you gonna do?"

"I'll tell them. I'll tell…" Who would she tell? Certainly not her mother. If anything that would just make things worse. "I'll tell the 911 lady."

He gripped her and lifted her up by the front of her shirt. His eyes had gone dark and stone-cold hard. "You do and you'll never see your baby sister again. I'll make sure if that." His boozy breath washed over her, and spittle sprayed her face. "Is that what you want, little girl? Because I'll make it happen. I promise you."

With a shove, he sent her flying across the room. Her head hit the wall and the world went dark. She didn't know how long she'd blacked out, but when she came to, June was huddled in the corner of her bed, trembling. Her father leaned over her, crooning those same words that haunted Megan's nightmares—" Such a pretty little girl. Daddy won't hurt you. I just want to hold you, that's all."

But Megan knew better. His belt was unbuckled, and he had that look on his face that chilled her to the bone. She let out a primal scream as a geyser of emotions flooded her body.

No, she couldn't let him hurt her sister. She wouldn't.

Megan jumped to her feet and grabbed the first thing she found on the dresser. It was a ceramic statue of Barney, the purple dinosaur June loved, and it was heavy.

She raised it high with two hands and brought it

down hard on the back of her father's head. The impact vibrated up her arms as she brought the statue down one, two, three times. "Leave. Her. Alone!"

Her father crumpled to the floor. Megan grabbed June's hand and pulled her off the bed. "Come on," she urged. "We have to go."

"Where, Meggy?" Tears were streaming down June's face.

"I don't know. But we have to get out of here before he wakes up." All Meg knew for sure was that she was the only one who could protect her baby sister. She took June's hand and pulled her out of the room. They raced through the living room where her mother was passed out, one arm hanging off the edge of the couch, still clutching a half-empty bottle.

Out the front door they went, through autumn leaves crunching underfoot. The sky was just getting dark as Megan led her sister into the nearby woods. There was a chill in the air, a chill that would get worse as the night deepened. Megan wished she'd thought to grab their jackets.

But they didn't run fast enough or far enough, and her sister's legs were too little to keep up. She plopped down on her bottom and let out a howl.

"Come on Buggy. We have to go." Megan tugged on her arm, but she didn't budge. She tried to pick her sister up, but she was too heavy.

"Don't wanna go no more. Want Mommy."

Too late. Megan heard their father coming up behind them. He grabbed Megan by the hair and jerked her off her feet. She shouted for her sister to run, but June sat frozen in fear, her eyes wide, her lips trembling. Their father hoisted them both up, one under each arm and dragged them home.

Chapter Thirty-Two

Present Day

Meg remembered everything now. She'd failed to protect her sister and in doing so had sealed her own fate. But she hadn't tried to hurt her. That was a lie her father had told to discredit her so no one would believe the truth. With the return of her memory, Meg realized that when her parents abandoned her at St. Ophelia's, it had left June unprotected. She couldn't imagine what her life must have been like. Every day since Meg suffered guilt about not protecting her sister from the same abuse she'd endured.

And yet none of that was in her journal. Had she suppressed the memory even then? Or had it simply been too painful to put down on paper?

The guilt and shame Meg had carried all her life was the major source of her depression. But it didn't have to be that way. She could rewrite her own story. Knowing that truth is what finally set Meg free.

****

It was important for Meg to talk to June first and explain everything she remembered. Only once those memories were untangled could she go to Ben with a clean slate.

One thing June had said stayed with her. "Was your fierce desire to protect me any different from

Ben's desire to protect you?"

Meg held that thought in her heart all the way home.

Home.

Ben met her at the door, his face shadowed with concern. "How did it go?"

Meg threw herself into his arms. "It all came back," she said. "All my memories. Oh Ben, I'm sorry for what I put you through. So much to tell you. I was never ever suicidal. I know that for sure now. And there's so much more."

She knew she was rambling but couldn't stop. There was so much to tell him. "My purse fell, and something rolled under the brake pedal. I couldn't stop. That's why there were no skid marks."

Ben wrapped his arms around her. "That was the one thing I couldn't explain. I felt so guilty. I thought it was my fault."

Meg was familiar with the feeling of guilt. Hadn't she lived with it all these years? "Not your fault. Not your fault at all. It really was an accident. I'd never try to kill myself."

With those words, she began the long process of unburdening herself. She recounted memories she hadn't thought about in ages. She explained how she'd been trying to save June, not hurt her. And all the guilt she'd lived with when she wasn't able to protect her baby sister.

She told Ben everything, including her history with Clay. "He's the one I was trying to call just before the accident. He was part of the reason I was afraid to get pregnant. After our fight, I realized I had to deal with our past before I could move forward. I know it was stupid, but it was important to put that behind me if we were to have a baby. And I did want to have your baby, Ben. I still do."

There was more, so much more she wanted to tell him, but they had the rest of their lives together. The most important thing she remembered was that it was Ben's stability that first appealed to her. He was grounded, stable, everything she wasn't. He was the kind of man she never thought she deserved.

He held her close. "Oh Meg. This is the happy ending I've always dreamed of. I couldn't have written it better myself."

Meg gave him a stern, but loving look. "I don't need you to write my happy ending, Ben. I can do it myself. I don't have to change my past as long as I'm in control of my present. *I* get to choose."

And she could. Meg realized that her strength came not in pretending her past didn't exist, but in overcoming the past and turning her scars into battle wounds.

Epilogue

The bookstore owner came up and shook Ben's hand. "Good to see you again. I have to tell you, there's a lot of buzz about this book already." He bent down and glanced at the baby in the stroller. "And who's this?"

"This is Carly," Ben said, beaming with pride. "Named after someone my wife said was like a mother to her."

"She looks just like you."

"Yeah, poor kid." His eyes held nothing but pure, unconditional love. "Imagine having a mother as beautiful as Meg and taking after your plain old dad?"

At the sound of Meg's name, they both glanced toward the front of the room. The store owner looked at his watch. "Guess it's about time to get started." He nudged Ben. "How does it feel to be on the other side of the table?"

"Feels good," Ben said. "Feels damn good."

He winked at Meg at the front of the room surrounded by her new book—*Letters from Gemma: a Tale of Truth, Love, and Transformation.* He gave her the thumbs up as she leaned into the microphone, cleared her head, and spoke.

"Hello," she said, her voice strong and clear. "My name is Meg Tyler, and this is my story."

A word about the author...

Linda Bleser began her writing career publishing short fiction for women's magazines. She writes heartwarming, powerful, thought-provoking women's fiction novels. A transplanted New Yorker, Linda and her husband have retired to sunny Florida where she continues to write on the beach or poolside. http://lindableser.com

Lightning Source UK Ltd.
Milton Keynes UK
UKHW021933030223
416465UK00023B/274